THE PLANETEERS

THE PLANETEERS

JOHN W. CAMPBELL, JR.

WILDSIDE PRESS

CONTENTS

THE BRAIN STEALERS OF MARS

I. IMITATION OF LIFE

Rod Blake looked up with a deep chuckle. The sky of Mars was almost black, despite the small, brilliant sun, and brighter stars and planets that shone visibly, Earth most brilliant of all, scarcely sixty million miles away.

"They'll have a fine time chasing us, back there, Ted." He nodded toward the brilliant planet.

Ted Penton smiled beatifically.

"They're probably investigating all our known haunts. It's their own fault if they can't find us—outlawing research on atomic power."

"They had some provocation, you must admit. Koelenberg should have been more careful. When a man takes off some three hundred square miles of territory spang in the center of Europe in an atomic explosion, you can't blame the rest of the world for being a bit skittish about atomic power research."

"But they might have had the wit to see that anybody that did get the secret would not wait around for the Atomic Power Research Death Penalty, but would light out for parts and planets quite unknown and leave the mess in the hands of a lawyer till the fireworks quieted down. It was obvious that when we developed atomic power we'd be the first men to reach Mars, and nobody could follow to bring us back unless they accepted the hated atomic power and used it," argued Blake.

"Wonder how old Jamison Montgomery Palborough made out with our claims," mused Penton. "He said he'd have it right in three months, and this is the third month and the third planet. We'll let the government stew, and sail on, fair friend, sail on. I still say that was a ruined city we saw as we landed."

"I think it was, myself, but I remember the way you did that kangaroo leap on your neck the first time you stepped out on the moon. You certainly saw stars."

"We're professionals at walking under cockeyed gravities now. Moon—Venus—"

"Yes, but I'm still not risking my neck on the attitude of a strange planet *and* a strange race at the same time. We'll investigate the planet a bit first, and yonder mudhole is the first stop. Come on."

They reached the top of one of the long rolling sand dunes and the country was spread out below them. It looked exactly as it had been from the last dune that they had struggled up, just as utterly barren, utterly bleak, and unendingly red. Like an iron planet, badly neglected and rusted.

The mudhole was directly beneath them, an expanse of red and brown slime, dotted here and there with clumps of dark red foliage.

"The stuff looks like Japanese maple," said Blake.

"Evidently doesn't use chlorophyll to get the sun's energy. Let's collect a few samples. You have your violet-gun and I have mine. I guess it's safe to split. There's a large group of things down on the left that look a little different. I'll take them while you go straight ahead. Gather any flowers, fruits, berries or seeds you see. Few leaves—oh, you know. What we got on Venus. General junk. If you find a small plant, put on your gloves and yank it out. If you see a big one, steer clear. Venus had some peculiarly unpleasant specimens."

Blake groaned. "You're telling me. I'm the bright boy that fell for that pretty fruit and climbed right up between the stems of a scissor tree. Uhuh. I shoot 'em down. Go ahead, and good luck."

Penton swung off to the left, while Blake slogged ahead to a group of weird-looking plants. They were dome-shaped things, three feet high, with a dozen long, drooping, sword-shaped leaves.

Cautiously Blake tossed a bit of stone into the center of one. It gave off a mournful, drumming boom, but the leaves didn't budge. He tried a rope on one leaf but the leaf neither stabbed, grabbed, or jerked away, as he had half expected after his lesson with the ferocious plants of Venus. Blake pulled a leaf off, then a few more. The plant acted quite plant-like, which pleasantly surprised him.

The whole region seemed seeded with a number of the things, nearly all about the same size. A few, sprinkled here and there, were in various stages of development, from a few protruding sword-leaves, to little three-inch domes on up to the full-grown plant. Carefully avoiding the larger ones, Rod plucked two small ones and thrust them into his specimen bag. Then he stood off and looked at one of the domes that squatted so dejectedly in the thick, gummy mud.

"I suppose you have some reason for being like that, but a good solid tree would put you all in the shade, and collect all the sunlight going. Which is little enough." He looked at them for some seconds picturing a stout Japanese maple in this outlandish red brown gum.

He shrugged, and wandered on, seeking some other plant. There were few others. Apparently this particular species throttled out other varieties very thoroughly. He wasn't very anxious anyway; he was much more interested in the ruined city they had seen from the ship. Ted Penton was cautious.

Eventually Blake followed his winding footsteps back toward the ship, and about where his footsteps showed he'd gathered his first samples, he stopped. There was a Japanese maple there. It stood some fifteen feet tall, and the bark was beautifully regular in appearance. The leaves were nearly a quarter of an inch thick, and arranged with a peculiar regularity, as were the branches. But it was very definitely a Japanese maple.

Rod Blake's jaw put a severe strain on the hinges thereof. It dropped some three inches, and Blake stared. He stared with steady, blank gaze at that perfectly impossible Japanese maple. He gawked dumbly. Then his jaw snapped shut abruptly, and he cursed softly. The leaves were stirring gently, and they were not a quarter of an inch thick. They were paper thin, and delicately veined. Further, the tree was visibly taller, and three new branches had started to sprout, irregularly now. They sprouted as he watched, growing not as twigs but as fully formed branches extending themselves gradually. As he stared harder at them they dwindled rapidly to longer twigs, and grew normally.

Rod let out a loud yip, and made tracks, rapidly extending themselves, toward the point where he'd last seen Ted Penton. Penton's tracks curved off, and Rod steamed down as fast as Mars' light gravity permitted, to pull up short as he rounded a corner of another sword-leaf dome clump. "Ted," he panted, "come over here. There's a—a—weird thing. A—it looks like a Japanese maple, but it doesn't. Because when you look at it, it changes."

Rod stopped, and started back, beckoning Ted.

Ted didn't move.

"I don't know what to say," he said quite clearly, rather panting, and sounding excited, though it was a quite unexciting remark, except for one thing. He said it in Rod Blake's voice!

Rod stiffened. Then he backed away hurriedly, stumbled over his feet and sat down heavily in the sand. "For the love of—Ted—Ted, wh-what did you s-s-say?"

"I don't know wh-what to s-s-say."

Rod groaned. It started out exactly like his own voice, changed rapidly while it spoke, and wound up a fair imitation of Ted's. "Oh, Lord," he groaned, "I'm going back to the ship. In a hurry."

He started away, then looked back over his shoulder. Ted Penton was moving now, swaying on his feet peculiarly. Delicately he picked up his left foot, shook it gently, like a man trying to separate himself from a piece of flypaper. Rod moved even more rapidly than he had before. Long, but rapidly shrinking roots dangled from the foot, gooey mud dropping from them as they shrank into the foot. Rod turned again with the violet-gun in his hand. It thrummed to blasting atomic energy, and a pencil beam of ravening ultra-violet fury shot out and a hazy ball of light surrounded it.

The figure of Ted Penton smoked suddenly, and a hole the size of a golf ball drove abruptly through the center of the head, to the accompaniment of a harsh whine of steam and spurts of oily smoke. The figure did not fall. It slumped. It melted rapidly, like a snowman in a furnace, the fingers ran together, the remainder of the face dropped, contracted, and became horrible. It was suddenly the face of a man whose pouched and dulled eyes had witnessed and enjoyed every evil the worlds knew, weirdly glowing eyes that danced and flamed for a moment in screaming fury of deadly hate—and dissolved with the last dissolution of the writhing face.

And the arms grew long, very long and much wider. Rod stood frozen while the very wide and rapidly widening arms beat up and down. The thing took off and flapped awkwardly away, and for an instant the last trace of the hate-filled eyes glittered again in the sun.

Rod Blake sat down and laughed. He laughed, and laughed again at the very funny sight of the melting face on the bat-bodied thing that had flown away with a charred hole in the middle of its grapefruit-sized head. He laughed even louder when another Ted-Penton-thing came around the corner of the vegetable clump, on the run. He aimed at the center of its head. "Fly away!" he yelled as he pressed the little button down.

This one was cleverer. It ducked. "Rod—for the love of—Rod, shut up," it said.

Rod stopped and considered slowly. This one talked with Ted Penton's voice. As it got up again he aimed more carefully and flashed again. He wanted it to fly away, too. It ducked again, in another direction this time, and ran in rapidly. Rod got up hastily and ran. He fell suddenly as some fibrous thing lashed out from behind and wrapped itself unbreakably about his arms and body, binding him helplessly.

Penton looked down at him, panting heavily.

"What's the trouble, Rod; and why in blazes were you shooting your gun at me?"

Rod heard himself laugh again, uncontrollably. The sight of Ted's worried face reminded him of the flying thing, with the melted face: Like an overheated wax figure. Penton reached out a deliberate hand and cracked him over the face, hard. In a moment Rod steadied, and Penton removed the noose from his arms and body. Blake sighed with relief.

"Thank God, it's you, Ted," he said. "Listen, I saw you—*you*—not thirty seconds ago. You stood over there, and I spoke to you. You answered in *my* voice. I started off, and your feet came up out of the ground with roots on them, like a plant's. I shot you through the forehead, and you melted down like a wax doll to a bat-thing that sprouted wings and flew away."

"Uhh—" said Penton soothingly. "Funny, at that. Why were you looking for me?"

"Because there's a Japanese maple where I was that grew while my back was turned, and changed its leaves while I looked at it."

"Oh, Lord," said Penton unhappily, looking at Rod. Then more soothingly, "I think we'd better look at it."

Rod led the way back on his tracks. When the maple should have been in sight, it wasn't at all. When they reached the spot where Rod's tracks showed it should have been, it wasn't there. There was only a somewhat wilted sword-bush. Rod stared blankly at it, then he went over and felt it cautiously. It remained placidly squatted, a slightly bedraggled lump of vegetation.

"That's where it was," said Blake dully. "But it isn't there any more. I know it was there."

"It must have been an—er—mirage," decided Penton. "Let's get back to the ship. We've had enough walking practice."

Rod followed him, wonderingly shaking his head. He was so wrapped up in his thoughts, that he nearly fell over Penton when Ted stopped with a soft, unhappy, gurgling noise. Ted turned around and looked at Rod carefully. Then he looked ahead again.

"Which," he asked at length, "is you?"

Rod looked ahead of Penton, over his shoulder. Another Rod was also standing in front of Penton. "My God," said Rod, "it's me this time!"

"I am, of course," said the one in front. It said it in Rod Blake's voice.

Ted looked at it, and finally shut his eyes.

"I don't believe it. Not at all. *Wo bist du gewesen, mein Freund?*"

"*Was sagst du?*" said the one in front. "But why the *Deutsch?*"

Ted Penton sat down slowly and thoughtfully. Rod Blake stared at Rod Blake blankly, slightly indignant.

"Let me think," said Penton unhappily. "There must be some way to tell. Rod went away from me, and then I come around the corner and find him laughing insanely. He takes a shot at me. But it looks, and talks like Rod. But he says crazy things. Then I go for a walk with him—or it—and meet another one that at least seems less insane than the first one. Well, well. I know German, of course, and so does Rod. Evidently this thing can read minds. Must be like a chameleon, only more so."

"What do you mean?" asked Rod Blake. It doesn't particularly matter which one.

"A chameleon can assume any color it wants to at will. Lots of animals have learned to imitate other animals for safety, but it takes them generations to do it. This thing, apparently, can assume any shape or color at will. A minute ago it decided the best form for the locality was a sword-bush. Some of these things must be real plants then. Rod thought of a maple tree, thought of the advantages of a maple tree, so it decided to try that, having read his mind. That was why it was wilted-looking; this isn't the right kind of country for maple trees. It lost water too fast. So it went back to the sword-bush.

"Now, this one has decided to try being Rod Blake, clothes and all. But I haven't the foggiest notion which one is Rod Blake. It won't do a bit of good to try him on languages we know, because he can read our minds. I know there must be some way. There must—there must—Oh yes. It's simple. Rod, just burn me a hole in that thing with your violet-gun."

Rod reached for his gun at once with a sigh of relief and triggered quickly. The phony Rod melted hastily. About half of it got down into the boiling mud before Rod incinerated the rest with the intense ultra-violet flare of the pistol. Rod sighed. "Thank the Lord it was me. I wasn't sure for a while, myself."

Ted shook himself, put his head in his hands, and rocked slowly. "By the Nine Gods of the Nine Planets, what a world! Rod, for the love of heaven, stay with me hereafter. Permanently. And whatever you do, don't lose that pistol. They can't grow a real violet-gun, but if they pick one up, may God help us. Let's get back to the ship, and away from this damned place. I thought you were mad. My error. It's just the whole bloody planet that's mad."

"I was—for a while. Let's move."

They moved. They moved hastily back across the sand dunes to the ship.

II. THE SECRET OF THE THUSHOL

"They're centaurs," gasped Blake. "Will you look at that one over there—a nice little calico. There's a beautiful little strawberry roan. What people! Wonder why the city is so dilapidated, if the people are still here in some numbers. Set 'er down, will you, Ted? They haven't anything dangerous, or they'd have a better city."

"Uhmmm—I suppose that's right. But I'd hate to have one of those fellows nudge me. They must weigh something noticeable, even here—about twelve hundred pounds back on Earth. I'm setting down in that square. You keep your hand on that ten-inch ion-gun while I step out."

The ship settled with a soft *thumpf* in the deep sandy dust of the ruined city square. Half a hundred of the centaurs were trotting leisurely up, with a grizzled old Martian in the lead, his mane sparse and coarse. Ted Penton stepped out of the lock.

"*Pholshth*," the Martian said after a moment's inspection. He extended his hands out horizontally from his shoulders, palms upward and empty.

"Friends," said Ted, extending his arms in a similar gesture, "I am Penton."

"Fasthun Loshthu," explained the centaur, indicating himself. "Penshun."

"He sounds like an ex-soldier," came Blake's voice softly. "Pension. Is he O.K.?"

"I think so. You can leave that post anyway, and shut off the main atomics, start auxiliary B, and close the rooms. Lock the controls with the combination and come on out. Bring your ion-gun as well as your ultra-violet. Lock the lock-doors."

"Blazes. I want to come out this afternoon. Oh well, O.K." Blake went to work hurriedly and efficiently. It was some thirty seconds before he was through in the power room. He stepped eagerly into the lock.

He stopped dead. Penton was on his back, moving feebly, the old centaur bent over him, with his long, powerful fingers fixed around the man's throat. Penton's head was shaking slowly back and forth on the end of his neck, in a loose, rather detached-looking way.

Blake roared and charged out of the lock, his two powerful pistols hastily restored to his holsters. He charged out—and sailed neatly over the centaur's back, underestimating Mars' feeble grip. In an instant he was on his feet again, and returning toward his friend when a skillful left forefoot caught his legs, and sent him tumbling as the heavy bulk of an agile young centaur landed on his back. Blake turned to see a smaller, lighter body far more powerfully muscled. In a moment, the Earthman broke the centaurs' grip and started through the six or seven others that surrounded him.

A grunted word of command dissolved the mêlée, and Blake stood up, leaping toward Penton.

Penton sat on the ground, rocking slowly back and forth, his head between his hands. "Oh, Lord, they all do it here."

"Ted—are you all right?"

"Do I sound it?" Penton asked unhappily. "That old bird just opened up my skull and poured a new set of brains in. Hypnotic teaching—a complete university education in thirty seconds—all done with hypnotism and no mirrors used. They have the finest education system. God preserve us from it."

"*Shthuntho ishthu thiu lomal?*" asked the old Martian pleasantly.

"*Ishthu psoth lonthul timul*," groaned Penton. "The worst of it is, it works. I know his language as well as I know English." Suddenly, he managed a slight grin. He pointed to Blake and said: "Blake *amo phusthu ptsoth*."

The old centaur's lined, sparsely bearded face smiled like a pleased child's. Blake looked at him uneasily.

"I don't like that fellow's fa—" He stopped, hypnotized. He walked toward the old Martian with blank eyes and the grace of an animated tailor's dummy. He lay down in sections, and the old Martian's long, supple fingers circled his neck. Gently, they massaged the back of his spine up to the base of his skull.

Penton smiled sourly from where he sat. "Oh, you don't like his face, eh? Wait and see how you like his system."

The centaur straightened. Slowly Blake sat up. His head continued to nod and weave in a detached sort of way, till he gingerly reached up, felt around for it and took it firmly in his hands. He rested his elbows on his knees.

"We didn't both have to know his blasted language," he managed bitterly at last. "Languages always did give me headaches, anyway."

Penton watched him unsympathetically.

"I hate repeating things, and you'll find it useful, anyway."

"You are from the third planet," the Martian stated politely.

Penton looked at him in surprise, started up, then rose to his feet gingerly.

"Get up slowly, Blake, I advise you for your own good." Then to the Martian: "Why, yes. But you knew! How?"

"My great-great grandfather told me of his trip to the third planet before he died. He was one of those that returned."

"Returned? You Martians have been to Earth?" gasped Blake.

"I guessed that," said Penton softly. "They're evidently the centaurs of legend. And I think they didn't go alone from this planet."

"Our people tried to establish a colony there, many, many years ago. It didn't succeed. They died of lung diseases faster than they could cross space. The main reason they went in the first place was to get away from the *thushol*. But the *thushol* simply imitated local Earth-animals and thrived. So the people came back. We built many ships, hoping that since we couldn't go, the *thushol* would. But they didn't like Earth." He shook his head sorrowfully.

"The *thushol*. So that's what you call 'em." Blake sighed. "They must be a pest."

"They were then. They aren't much any more."

"Oh, they don't bother you any more?" asked Penton.

"No," said the old centaur apathetically. "We're so used to them."

"How do you tell them from the thing they're imitating?" Penton asked grimly. "That's what I need to know."

"It used to bother us because we couldn't," Loshthu said, "but it doesn't any more."

"I know—but how do you tell them apart? Do you do it by mind-reading?"

"Oh, no. We don't try to tell them apart. That way they don't bother us any more."

Penton looked at Loshthu thoughtfully for some time. Blake rose gingerly, and joined Penton in his enwrapped contemplation of the grizzled Martian. "Uhmmmm," said Penton at last, "I suppose that is one way of looking at it. I should think it would make business rather difficult though. Also social relations, not knowing whether it was your wife or just a real good imitation."

"I know. We found it so for many years," Loshthu agreed. "That was why our people wanted to move to Earth. But later they found that three of the ship commanders were *thushol*, so the people came back to Mars where they could live at least as easily as the *thushol*."

Penton mentally digested this for some moments, while the half hundred centaurs about stood patiently, apathetically motionless.

"We have myths on Earth of centaurs, people like you, and of magic creatures who seemed one thing, but when captured became snakes or tigers or other unpleasant beasts, but if held long enough reverted to human shape and would then grant a wish. Yes, the *thushol* are intelligent; they could have granted a simple Earth barbarian's wish."

Loshthu shook his head slowly.

"They are not intelligent, I believe. Maybe they are. But they have perfect memories for detail. They would imitate one of our number, attend our schools, and so learn all we knew. They never invented anything for themselves."

"What brought about the tremendous decline in your civilization? The *thushol*?"

The centaur nodded.

"We forgot how to make space ships and great cities. We hoped that would discourage the *thushol* so that they would leave us. But they forgot, too, so it didn't help."

"Good Lord," Blake said, "how in the name of the Nine Planets do you live with a bunch like that?"

Loshthu looked at Blake slowly.

"Ten," he said. "Ten planets. You can't see the tenth with any practicable instrument till you get out beyond Jupiter. Our people discovered it from Pluto."

Blake stared at him owlishly. "But how can you live with this gang? With a civilization like that—I should think you'd have found some means of destroying them."

"We did. We destroyed all the *thushol*. Some of the *thushol* helped us, but we thought that they were our own people. It happened because a very wise, but very foolish philosopher calculated how many *thushol* could live parasitically on our people. Naturally the *thushol* took his calculations to heart. Thirty-one percent of us are *thushol*."

Blake looked around with a swiftly unhappy eye.

"You mean—some of these here are *thushol*?" he asked.

Loshthu nodded.

"Always. They reproduced very slowly at first, in the form of an animal that was normally something like us, and reproduced as did other animals. But then they learned to imitate the amoebas when they studied in our laboratories. Now they simply split. One big one will split into several small ones, and each small one will eat one of the young of our people, and take its place. So we never know which is which. It used to worry us." Loshthu shook his head slowly.

Blake's hair rose slightly away from his head, and his jaw dropped away. "My God," he gasped. "Why didn't you do something?"

"If we killed one we suspected, we might be wrong, which would kill our own child. If we didn't, and just believe it our own child anyway, it at least gave us the comfort of believing it. And if the imitation is so perfect one can't tell the difference, what is the difference?"

Blake sat down again, quietly.

"Penton," he sighed, at length, "those three months are up, let's get back to Earth—fast."

Penton looked at him. "I wanted to a long time back. Only I thought of something else. Sooner or later, some other man is going to come here with atomic power, and if he brings some of those *thushol* back to Earth with him, accidentally, thinking it's his best friend—well, I'd rather kill my own child than live with one of those, but I'd rather not do either. They can reproduce as fast as they can eat, and if they eat like an amoeba—God help us. If you maroon one on a desert island, it will turn into a fish, and swim home. If you put it in jail it will turn into a snake and go down the drain pipe. If you dump it in the desert, it will turn into a cactus and get along real nice, thank you."

"Good God."

"And they won't believe us, of course. I'm sure as blazes not going to take one back to prove it. I'll just have to get some kind of proof from this Loshthu."

"I hadn't thought of that. What can we get?"

"All I can think of is to see what they can let us have, then take all we can, and make a return trip with reputable and widely believed zoologists and biologists to look into this thing. Evolution has produced some weird freaks, but this is a freakier weirdness than has ever been conceived."

"I still don't really believe it," Blake said. "The only thing I am firmly convinced of is my headache."

"It's real enough and logical enough. Logical as hell. And hell on Earth if they ever get there. Evolution is always trying to produce an animal that can survive anywhere, conquer all enemies, the fittest of the surviving fit. All life is based on one thing: protoplasm. Basically, it's the same in every creature, every living thing, plant and animal, amoeba and man. It is just modified slightly, hooked together in slightly different ways. The *thushol* are built of protoplasm—but infinitely more adaptable protoplasm. They can do something about it, make it take the form of a bone cell and be part of a thigh bone, or be a nerve cell in a brain. From some of that ten-second-college-course Loshthu poured into me, I gather that at first the *thushol* were good imitations outside, but if you cut into one, you could see that the organs weren't there. Now they have everything. They went through Martian medical colleges, of course, and know all about what makes a centaur tick, and so they make themselves with the same kind of tickers. Oh, very nice."

"They don't know much about us. Maybe with the X-ray fluoroscope screen we could have told those imitations of us," suggested Blake.

"Oh, no, by no means. If we knew the right form, they'd read it in our minds, and have it. Adaptive protoplasm. Just think, you couldn't kill it in an African jungle, because when a lion came along, it would be a little, lady lion, and when an elephant showed up, it would be a helpless baby elephant. If a snake bit it, I suppose the damned thing would turn into something immune to snake bites—a tree, or something like that. I just wonder where it keeps the very excellent brain it evidently has."

"Well, let's find out what Loshthu can offer us by way of proofs."

III. MIND-READERS AND COMPANY

It developed that Martians had once had museums. They still had them, because nobody was sufficiently interested to disturb their age-long quiet. Martians lived centuries, and their memories were long; but once or twice in a lifetime did a Martian enter the ancient museums.

Penton and Blake spent hours in them, intensive hours under Loshthu's guidance. Loshthu had nothing but time, and Penton and Blake didn't want to linger. They worked rapidly, collecting thin metal sheaves of documents, ancient mechanisms, a thousand things. They baled them with rope that they had brought from the ship when they moved it nearer the museum. Finally, after hours of labor, bleary-eyed from want of sleep, they started out again to the ship.

They stepped out of the gloomy dusk of the museum into the sun-lit entranceway. Immediately, from behind a dozen pillars, a leaping, flashing group of men descended upon them, tore the books, the instruments, the data sheaves from their hands. They were upset, slugged, trampled on and spun around. There were shouts and cries and curses.

Then there was silence. Twelve Pentons and thirteen Blakes sat, lay or stood about on the stone stairway. Their clothes were torn, their faces and bodies bruised, there was even one black eye, and another developing swiftly. But twelve Pentons looked exactly alike, each clasping a bit of data material. Thirteen Blakes were identical, each carrying a bit of factual mustiness under his arm or in his hand.

Loshthu looked at them, and his lined, old face broke into a pleased smile. "Ah," he said. "There are more of you. Perhaps some can stay with us to talk now."

Penton looked up at Loshthu, all the Pentons did. Penton was quite sure he was *the* Penton, but he couldn't think of any way to prove it. It was fairly evident that *thushol* had decided to try Earth again. He began to wonder just—

"Loshthu, just why," asked one of the Pentons in Penton's voice, "did the *thushol* not stay on Earth if they could live there?"

Penton was quite sure he had been the one to think of that partic—

"Pardon me, but wasn't that the question I was going to ask?" said another Penton in well-controlled fury. Penton smiled gently. It seemed evident that—

"I can apparently be spared the trouble of doing my own talking. You all help so," said one of the numerous Pentons angrily.

"Say, how in hell are we going to tell who's who?" demanded one of the Blakes abruptly.

"That damned mind-thief stole my question before I had a chance—"

"Why you—you—you talking! I was just about—"

"I think," said one of the Pentons wearily, "you might as well stop getting peeved, Blake, because they'll all act peeved when you do. What do you know. I beat all my imitators to the draw on that remark. A noble achievement, you'll find, Rod. But you might just as well pipe down, and I'll pipe down, and we'll see what our good friend, Loshthu, has to say."

"Eh," sighed Loshthu. "You mean about the *thushol* leaving Earth? They did not like it. Earth is a poor planet, and the people were barbarians. Evidently they are not so now. But the *thushol* do not like work, and they found richer sustenance on Mars."

"I thought so," said Penton. (Does it matter which one?) "They've decided that Earth is richer than Mars now, and want a new host. Don't draw that pistol, Blake! Unfortunately, my friend, we had twenty-five ion-guns and twenty-five violet-guns made up. If we'd had more we would have more companions. We were exceedingly unfortunate in equipping ourselves so well in the matter of clothing, and being so thoughtful as to plan all of it right, so we carried a lot of each of the few kinds. Exceedingly. However, I think we can improve things a little bit. I happen to remember that one ion-gun is out of commission, and I had the coils out of two of the violet-guns to repair them. That makes three guns out of service. We will each stand up and fire, one at a time, at the sand in front there. The line forms on the right."

The line formed. "Now," continued that particular Penton, "we will each fire, beginning with myself, one at a time. First ion, then violet. When one of us evidences lack of a serviceable gun, the others will join in removing him rapidly but carefully. Are we ready? Yes?" That Penton held up his ion-gun, and pushed the button.

It didn't fire, and immediately the portico stank with his smoke.

"That's one," said the next Penton. He raised his ion-gun and fired. Then his violet-gun. Then he raised it and fired again, at a rapidly dissolving Blake. "That makes two. That one evidently found, when we fired at the first one, that his didn't work. We have one more to eliminate. Next?"

Presently another Blake vanished. "Well, well," said Penton pleasantly, "the Blake-Penton odds are even. Any suggestions?"

"Yes," said Blake tensely. "I've been thinking of a patch I put in one suit that I ripped on Venus." Another Blake vanished under the mutual fire.

"There's one thing I want to know. Why in blazes are those phonies so blasted willing to kill each other, and though they know which is which, don't kill us? And how did they enter the ship?" Rod demanded. Or at least a Rod.

"They," said two Pentons at once. Another one looked at them. "Bad timing, boys. Rodney, my son, we used a combination lock. These gentlemen are professional mind-readers. Does that explain their possession of the guns? I've been thinking right along of one way to eliminate these excessive excrescences, consisting of you going into a huddle with your tribe, and eliminating all but the one you know to be yourself, and I doing the same. Unfortunately, while they're perfectly willing to kill each other so long as they don't die, they will prevent their own deaths by adequate, unfortunately adequate defense.

"Now since these little gun tests and others have been made I think it fairly evident that we are not going to leave this planet until the two right men are chosen and only two go into that ship with us. Fortunately they can't go without us, because while they can read minds, it takes more than knowledge to navigate a space ship, at least such knowledge as they can get from us. It takes understanding, which mere memory will not supply. They need us.

"We will, therefore, march dutifully to the ship, and each of us will replace his guns carefully in the prepared racks. I know that I'm the right Penton—but you don't. So no movement will be made without the unanimous agreement of all Pentons and Blakes."

Blake looked up, white-faced.

"If this wasn't so world-shakingly serious, it would be the damnedest comic opera that ever happened. I'm afraid to give up my gun."

"If we all give them up, I think it puts us even. We have some advantage in that they don't want to kill us, and if worse comes to worst, we could take them to Earth, making damned sure that they didn't get away. On Earth we could have protoplasmic tests made that would tell the story. By the way, that suggests something. Yes indeed, I think we can make tests here. Let us repair to this ship."

IV. PENTON'S STRATEGY

The Blakes sat down and stayed down. "Ted, what in blazes can we do?" His voice was almost tearful. "You can't tell one of these ghastly things from another. You can't tell one from me. We can't—"

"Oh, God," said another Blake, "that's not me. That's just another one of those damned mind-stealers."

Another one groaned hopelessly.

"That wasn't either." They all looked helplessly at the line of Pentons. "I don't even know who's my friend."

Penton nodded. All the Pentons nodded, like a grotesquely solemn chorus preparing to recite some blessing. They smiled in superhuman unity. "That's all right," they said in perfect harmony. "Well, well. A new stunt. Now we all talk together. That makes things easier. I think there may be a way to tell the difference. But you must absolutely trust me, Blake. You must give up your guns, putting all faith in my ability to detect the right one, and if I'm wrong, realize that I will not know. We can try such simple tests as alcohol, whiskey, to see if it makes them drunk, and pepper to see if it burns their tongues—"

"It won't work," said Blake tensely. "Lord, Penton, I can't give up my guns—I won't—"

Penton, all the Pentons smiled gently. "I'm half again as fast as you are, Blake, and no Martian-born imitation of you is going to be faster. Maybe these Martian imitations of me are as fast as I am. But you know perfectly well that I could ray the whole gang of you, all ten of you, out of existence before any one of you could move a finger. You know that, don't you, Rod?"

"Lord, yes, but Ted, Ted, don't do that—don't make me give up my guns—I've got to keep them. Why should I give up mine, if you keep yours?"

"That probably was not you speaking, Rod, but it doesn't matter. If it wasn't what you thought, we could do something about it. Therefore, that is what you wanted to say, just as this is what I wanted to say, whether I said it or not. Oh, Lord preserve us. It talks with my voice! But anyway, the situation is this; one of us has to have unquestioned superiority over the other gang. Then, the one with the whip hand can develop proof of identity, and enforce his decisions. As it is, we can't."

"Let me be the one, then," snapped one Blake.

"I didn't mean that," sighed another. "That wasn't me."

"Yes it was," said the first. "I spoke without thinking. Go ahead. But how are you going to make the others give up their guns? I'm willing. You can't make them?"

"Oh, yes I can. I have my faithful friends, here," said Penton grimly, his eleven hands waving to his eleven counterparts. "They agree with me this far, being quite utterly selfish."

"But what's your system. Before I put my neck in the noose, I have to know that noose isn't going to tighten on it."

"If I had a sound system in mind—I'm carefully refraining from developing one—they'd read it, weigh it, and wouldn't agree at all. They still have hopes. You see that pepper and alcohol system won't work perfectly because they can read in my mind the proper reaction, and be drunk, or have an inflamed tongue at will, being perfect actors. I'm going to try just the same. Rod, if you ever trusted me, trust me now."

"All right, come on. We'll go to the ship, and any one of these things that doesn't part with its gun is *not* me. Ray it."

Blake rose jerkily, all ten of him, and went down to the ship.

The Pentons followed faithfully after. Abruptly Penton rayed one Blake. His shoulder blades had humped curiously and swiftly. Wings were developing. "That helps," said Penton, holstering his guns.

The Blakes went on, white-faced. They put the weapons in the racks in the lock stoically. The Martians had seen to them, inconceivably swift movements of Penton's gun hands, and Penton knew that he, himself, had done the raying that time. But he still didn't know a way to prove it without causing a general mêlée which would bring about their own deaths. That wasn't so important. The trouble was that given fifty years, the rest of the world would descend on this planet unwarned. Then all Earth would be destroyed. Not with flame and sword and horrible casualty lists, but silently and undetectably.

The Blakes came out, unarmed. They shuffled and moved about uneasily, tensely, under the watchful eyes of eleven Pentons armed with terrifically deadly weapons.

Several Pentons went into the ship, to come out bearing pepper, saccharine tablets, alcohol, the medicine chest. One of them gathered them together and looked them over. "We'll try pepper," he said, rather unhappily. "Line up."

The Blakes lined up, hesitantly. "I'm putting my life in your hands, Ted," said two of them in identical, plaintive tones.

Four Pentons laughed shortly. "I know it. Line up. Come and get it."

"First," he sighed, after a moment, "stick out the tongue, patient."

With unsteady hands he put a bit of pepper from the shaker on the fellow's tongue. The tongue snapped in instantly, the Blake clapped his hands to his mouth, gurgling unpleasantly. "Waaaar!" he gasped. "Waar—achooo—damnt!"

With hands like flashing light, Penton pulled his own, and a neighbor's ion-gun. In a fiftieth of a second all but the single gagging, choking, coughing Blake were stinking, smoking, swiftly dissolving and flowing rubbish. The other Penton methodically helped destroy them.

Blake stopped gagging in surprise.

"My God, it might not have been the right one!" he gasped.

The ten Pentons sighed softly. "That finally proves it. Thank God. Definitely. That leaves me to find. And it won't work again, because while you can't read my mind to find the trick that told, these brothers of mine have. The very fact that you don't know how I knew, proves that I was right."

Blake stared at him dumbly. "I was the first one—" he managed between a cough and a sneeze.

"Exactly. Go on inside. Do something intelligent. Use your head. See what you can think of to locate me. You have to use your head in some such way that they don't mind-read it first, though. Go ahead."

Blake went, slow-footed. The first thing he did was to close the lockdoor, so that he was safely alone in the ship. Blake went into the control room, donned an air-suit complete with helmet, and pushed a control handle over. Then a second. Presently he heard curious bumpings and thumpings, and strange floppings and whimperings. He went back rapidly, and rayed a supply chest and two crates of Venusian specimens that had sprouted legs and were rapidly growing arms to grasp ray pistols. The air in the ship began to look thick and greenish; it was colder.

Contentedly Blake watched, and opened all the room doors. Another slithering, thumping noise attracted him, and with careful violet-gun work he removed an unnoticed, extra pipe that was crawling from the crossbrace hangers. It broke up into lengths that rolled about unpleasantly. Rod rayed them till the smallest only, the size of golf balls with curious blue-veined legs, staggered about uncertainly. Finally even they stopped wriggling.

Half an hour Rod waited, while the air grew very green and thick. Finally to make sure he started some other apparatus, and watched the thermometer go down, down till moisture grew on the walls and became frost, and no more changes took place. Then he went around with an opened ion-gun with a needle beam and poked everything visible with it.

The suction fans cleared out the chlorine-fouled atmosphere in two minutes, and Blake sat down wearily. He flipped over the microphone switch and spoke into the little disc. "I've got my hand on the main ion-gun control. Penton, I love you like a brother, but I love Earth more. If you can induce your boy friends to drop their guns in a neat pile and retire—O.K. If not, and I mean if not within thirty seconds, this ion-gun is going into action and there won't be any more Pentons. Now, drop!"

Grinning broadly, with evident satisfaction, ten Pentons deposited twenty heart-cores of ultra-essence of destruction, and moved off. "Way off," said Blake grimly. They moved.

Blake collected twenty guns. Then he went back into the ship. There was a fine laboratory at one end, and with grim satisfaction, he took down three cotton-stoppered tubes, being very careful to handle them with rubber gloves. "You never did man a good turn before, tetanus, but I hope you spread high, wide and handsome here—"

He dumped them into a beaker of water, and took beaker and glass down to the lock and out. The ten waited at a distance.

"All right, Penton. I happen to know you took a shot of tetanus anti-vaccine some while ago, and are immune. Let's see if those blasted brain-stealers can steal the secret of something we know how to make, but don't know anything about. They can gain safety by turning into a chicken, which is immune, but not as human creatures. That's a concentrated dose of tetanus. Go drink it. We can wait ten days if we have to."

Ten Pentons marched boldly up to the beaker, resting beside the ship. One stepped forward to the glass—and nine kept right on stepping. They stepped into the lee of the ship where the ion-gun could not reach.

Blake helped Penton into the ship with a broad grin.

"Am I right?"

"You're right," sighed Penton, "but God knows why. You can't get tetanus by swallowing it, and lockjaw doesn't develop so quickly as ten days."

"I didn't know for sure." Blake grinned. "They were too busy trying to find out what I was doing to follow your mind. Ah—there they go. Will you ray them or shall I?" asked Blake politely, sighting the ion-gun at the nine flapping, rapidly vanishing things scuttling across the red, rusty planet. The ship dipped sharply in pursuit. "There's one thing"—he straightened as the incredible glare died in thin air—"I want to know. How in blazes did you pick me out?"

"To do what you did requires some five hundred different sets of muscles in a beautifully coordinated neuro-muscular hookup, which I didn't believe those things could imitate without a complete dissection. I took the chance it was you."

"Five hundred sets of muscles! What the heck did I do?"

"You sneezed."

Rod Blake blinked slowly, and slowly his jaw tested again its supports and their flexibility.

THE DOUBLE MINDS

I. PRISONERS ON GANYMEDE

"P'holkuun's coming back," Ted Penton sighed. "Maybe he meant it."

Rod Blake stirred restlessly on the bunk.

"Will you make your news reports more explicit? You have your mug against the only clear spot on the damn glass door. Which one of those animated beanpoles is P'holkuun?"

"How can I describe him? He's a Ganymedian jailer, to you. They all look alike. Since we are the first human beings ever to see Ganymedians—or Ganymede itself—there aren't any words in the language to describe him. He is seven feet three inches tall, weighs about one hundred and fifty—or he would on Earth. He has that attractive green hair they all have, and he is wearing a Shaloor guard's uniform. He is shooing away our other guard."

"I guess he is as good an orator as you were," Blake grunted. "In five minutes you learned their language, found his political opinions, and had him sold on you to start a revolution. Man, you are political dynamite!"

"Political atomic power," Penton replied sourly. "I got us kicked out of Earth first for experimenting with the stuff. Kick number one; we get in the soup on Mars. Head for home, and all Earth turns out a great welcome for us—twenty-one gun salutes. Only they forgot to take out the sixteen-inch shells. They still don't want us. It was easier here. P'holkuun's a member of the rebel party, and the mind-reading stunt I learned from the Martians helped me make friends with him."

"Penton," suddenly whispered the thin, squeaky voice of the friendly jailer outside, "the Shaloor have investigated your spaceship again. They are afraid."

"They are wise," replied Penton grimly. "If they disturb the atomic balances I have established in the engines, they'll blow this whole satellite clear out of Jupiter's system. They haven't a glimmering of an idea what forces I use."

"They don't believe you. They say you are a liar." The jailer, a Lanoor, sounded doubtful himself.

"They wanted me to take them in it out into space," went on Penton. "If they know more about my machine than I do, why don't they build one like it, and go out in their own machine? You don't even have the words atomic power and electricity in your language."

P'holkuun shook his head slowly.

"You do not understand. Ten years ago, the first Shaloor was made. He a Lanoor, but he invented an operation, and tried it on a friend, then the friend did it to him. The brain is divided into two halves, only one of which ever works in thinking. If, however, a man is injured so the half he is using is destroyed, then the other half works. The Shaloor found out how to make both halves work at once. The brain is made up of thousands and thousands of individual cells, each one helping to think. When the Shaloor doubled the number of thinking cells that work, he became, not twice as brilliant, but over ten thousand times as keen-minded. With two factors, A and B, you can make only two combinations: AB and BA. With twice as many factors, you can make far more than twice as many combinations.

"In ten short years the Shaloor overthrew our rulers, developed a new civilization. They invented the *shleath*, and a thousand new vegetables and new animal foods. They will be able to learn your secret shortly. Some day our rebellion may succeed."

"The Shaloor are not omniscient. You are needlessly afraid of them." Penton snapped.

The Lanoor's big, broad face split in a slow grin.

"You are in jail, Urd-mahn, thanks to the Shaloor."

"They trapped us by treachery—"

"The Shaloor are always treacherous. It is intelligent they say."

"They will find it most unintelligent when my people come ten months from now with ships that can wipe out this city in a moment's time. We will so disturb the Shaloor that your waiting rebellion can succeed." Their jailer did not know that they had been exiled from Earth.

"Their gas—their gas always stops us. And the *shleath*. No man can face that—" The guard's ruddy face went pale at the thought, and Penton cursed silently that his very fear made his mind unreadable, even to the ancient method the Martians had learned and recorded ten thousand years ago in the ancient museums he had recently plundered. He could only catch vague, formless jellies wavering in a cloudiness of fear as the mental image.

"We have an older knowledge," Penton said shortly. "But do as you will. We will be out in a day's time, if the Shaloor have not first released the frightful energies of our ship in their blunderings."

"I—I will talk with my comrades tonight," P'holkuun said, and moved down the corridor uneasily. Penton turned away from the little window in the frosted glass of the door. Though his Earth-bred strength was five times that of a Ganymedian, it was still far less than was needed to break down the thick, tough glass. Penton looked at it disgustedly.

"Damn," he complained mournfully.

"I take it he said, 'No.' " Blake looked morosely at the door. "Nice birds they have here. You greet 'em friendly, they wave and grin, and beckon from airplanes while you come down out of space. You step out—and plunko—they trap you with glass bombs of sleep-gas. Ah, well—I can't sleep, I can't smoke, and I can't move. I—"

"Oh, shut up. Here, I'll make you sleep. Hypnotism."

"Can you? Say—that's right, you learned a lot of dope from those Martian records. Go ahead." Blake lay back thankfully. Ten seconds later he realized his error. He was helplessly hypnotized, and already he recognized the flood of strange thoughts pouring into his mind, other-worldly ideas. Penton was giving him knowledge of the Lanoorian language by the technique the Martians had developed ten thousand years ago: hypnotic teaching.

Blake was about to acquire a complete understanding of Lanoor, in about five minutes. Also, all the headaches that he would normally have had learning a language would be equally concentrated into one great-granddaddy of all headaches. He struggled to free his will—

* * * *

The sun was shining in through the whole rear wall of the cell, which meant that it was day again, and he had slept for hours.

"No," said Penton's voice. But it was Lanoor he was speaking, and Blake moved his head gingerly and groaned audibly. Yes, the headache was there.

"No, I'll have to make the medicine myself. Tell them Blake is dying, that the air does not suit him. Hear him moan? Tell the Shaloor that I must have that stuff."

Blake saw a shadow, distorted by the uneven glass of the prison wall, move off. Penton turned toward him.

"Excellent, Rod, excellent. Nothing could have been better timed. I didn't know you were awake; and your help was really welcome."

"Help? Help, you cosmic blight! My head."

"I know. But we needed the stuff. Now he'll get it for us. You know their language now—we'll get the stuff I want."

"I've got a headache. Go away and shut up. Oh-h-h."

* * * *

He dozed, for when he opened his eyes again, his head pained less, and Penton was hard at work with some glass flasks, pungently odorous liquids, and various powders.

"Will you groan?" asked Penton pleasantly. "The guard is watching and listening."

Blake obliged. "Oh-h-h—what in double blazes—ah-h-h-h—are you stewing? It smells like fury!"

"I'm too busy trying to figure out something. Keep groaning, by the way. This is medicine for you. You're suffering because the atmosphere doesn't suit you. I can stand it, because I've had a dose of this atmospheric-cosmic-telluric acclimatizer."

"Groan? Great God, if it's anything you cooked up, I'm going to recover right here and now. You're no medicine man!"

"I am now. The stuff is now prepared. Hm-m-m—" he passed it under his nose. A mixture of pleasant, fruity smells, and peculiarly rank, acrid odors pervaded the room. From a bottle he measured out a number of gritty crystals, then from a second bottle of green glass, a few more. He sniffed the results, tasted it.

"Try a bit." He grinned at last, and passed it over. "Guaranteed to make you lick tigers like lollypops."

Blake took it at arm's length, and sniffed. His eyes widened. He tasted it. His mouth widened in a grin.

"What stuff! Happy days will come again." A considerable portion of the potent brew went down. Blake relinquished it only under protest. "All right, but explain the ingredients."

Penton helped himself to a bit, and nodded.

"Citric acid—crystallized acid of lemon. Sucrose—commonly sold under the name of sugar. Ethanol—otherwise ethyl alcohol. Carbonic acid—in no way related to the one with an 'l' in it—better liked as soda water. I thought the combine might strike you where you needed it, and anyway, I needed the rest of the brew."

Penton looked at, but did not handle, a large flask in which a watery liquid was stirring slowly about a white powder. Fully a gallon of the stuff was there already, and he cautiously added more from a large beaker, and more powder from a glass bottle.

"And that?" asked Blake.

"The universal solvent. Anyway, it should get us out of here, I believe. I—"

With a soft clank, the large glass block disintegrated, and its contents spewed out over the metal table, and down the glass wall of the cell. The table had been in a corner, and the adjacent walls and floor were liberally flooded with the deluge. An intense, suffocating odor sprang up at once. Blake pulled his feet off the floor hastily, and looked in dismay at Penton.

"I thought it would," Penton sighed. "It does that."

"What?"

"Be patient and we'll see. You are supposed to be recovering from a fatal illness. I've got to tell the guard it's according to plan."

The guard was already unlocking the door, for he had seen the deluge. Penton waved his hands.

"Keep out—the vapors—Blake must breathe the vapors!"

The unsuspecting guard had the door somewhat open, but getting the said vapors himself, he promptly decided that Blake was welcome to them and departed.

"Look, Rod, they have just turned on the corridor lights!" explained Penton.

"Which reminds me to ask why you said even before we landed, that they didn't have electricity. Those may not be electric gas-glow tubes, but they're certainly one swell imitation."

Penton laughed. "Wrong, two out of two. I said they didn't have electricity before we landed because the instruments on the ship indicated no sign of electric or electromagnetic energy of any sort produced by man on the whole planet. As for the lamps, electric gas-glow tubes are a poor imitation of *them*. Those are biological lamps. They use some kind of a bacterial ferment, and they turn them on by letting air into them. Notice how dark it is already? Small world turning rapidly on its axis, with a thin atmosphere. It will be dark in another quarter hour. Better pack your belongings, because, m' lad, we are going out."

"How? Did P'holkuun finally decide to throw in with us?"

"No, not yet, anyway. I didn't think he would until we got out of here on our own legs. P'holkuun isn't going to ask help from somebody who is tied worse than he is. But—he'll help plenty once we get out of here."

"Yes—but how? Don't tell me we can go out through those solid walls!"

"Yes, through the walls. It's dark enough now, I suppose. Rod, will you wield that hefty hoof of yours against the wall in the neighborhood of that table, while I obscure the window in the door? I would have a chat with our jailer. Don't shake the building, though. You should go right through the wall. Easy."

Blake moved the table. Penton's argument with the jailer was about something impossible, and very loud, but Blake paid little attention because of the way the wall was acting. The clear, hard glass was crumbling under his foot into sand. It broke out in great chunks, and crumbled as though his foot were a pile-driver. In utter surprise he felt his boot sink into the stuff—and through it! In almost no time, Penton had so annoyed the jailer that the man walked down the corridor to avoid Penton's voice, and Penton walked with Blake through the wall of the prison.

"Jupiter will rise in about two hours. When he comes up you won't need to be told, but you will need to be hidden," said Penton. "We appear to the local populace as inconspicuous as a pair of orangutans walking down Fifth Avenue arm in arm. And slightly less harmless. To them our build is the quintessence of horrible, brute strength.

"So when Jupiter's great bulk comes over the horizon, the reflected light is going to make us conspicuous, and not a sight to calm the nerves of nice, old Lanoorian ladies. Further, thanks to P'holkuun's thoughts, I know that our ship is somewhere on the far side of the city. So come on. First we have to get away from this neighborhood."

II. THE DOUGHBALLS

Ted Penton sailed over a twenty-foot wall surrounding the jail, and Blake found it easy to follow because of the satellite's low gravity.

"What"—he panted after a moment—"is the secret—of the wall—stop running—you fool—I'm winded."

"The air's too thin—to keep—it up," agreed Penton. In the darkness of a tiny alleyway they stopped. "The stuff I used was crotonaldehyde—an organic liquid—derivable from—alcohol. Works on the fact—that glass is not a true—solid."

Blake stared at him, panting.

"Yeah. Stone walls do—not a prison make—nor iron bars a cage. So what is it? That glass wall looked solid enough—it had me bluffed."

"Puffed, did you say? Glass is a liquid. Liquid got so cold it has turned stiff—past the gooey stage. Crotonaldehyde has the curious property of turning it solid. Long heating and cooling does it too, that's why kerosene lamp-chimneys used to get so fragile. Solid glass is extremely brittle and as strong as so much sand. When that stuff turned it solid it took all the strength out of it. We have to steal a car. Damn. No running or we will pant so loud they'll hear us a block away. They have cars. There ought to be one around here somewhere, and let us pray they haven't invented locks for 'em."

They covered six blocks before they saw a rounded, bulky lump in the road that was evidently an automobile.

"You drive, Rod," Penton said softly. "You are a better driver than I, and a better mechanic. Can you figure it out?"

"Lord, help us, no! Is it electric? No. Steam? Compressed air? Gasoline? Diesel? How in blazes should I know? Where's the engine? Both ends look alike. I have never seen anybody drive one, and I don't even know which end is front. Is this one a steering lever, and—well, what's that other one back there? I—" the car jerked ahead suddenly.

"Oh," said Penton, "you do know how to start it."

Blake was too busy hanging on. He held the lever grimly in his hand, and pulled.

"What do I do to stop it?" He tried pushing the lever. The car showed capabilities of speed. He pressed in a different direction. The car stopped accelerating but by no means slowed down. The quite accidental fact that the road was straight helped. His foot felt feverishly for a brake pedal—and the car swerved aside into a pole.

"I think," said Penton, bending the door frame out of his way, "that they probably have a more comfortable, if no more effective means of stopping them. They can't have light poles everywhere. We had better hurry elsewhere. Someone will certainly investigate that crash. Anyway, the next car we try, you'll know they steer with their feet, and not try to jam on the brakes with the steering gear."

"The next one," said Blake clearly, "you will know they steer with their feet. And I'm going to take time out to find out how in blazes they work. I just took hold of that handle—and away she went. No starter—nothing!"

Six blocks away they found another car, not exactly like the first, but similar, seven seats instead of five. Blake looked at Penton.

Penton hesitated, and looked about him. Surrounding warehouses loomed, dark masses against a star-studded sky. A tiny, bright moon rode high in the sky, and lower was another, even smaller. Giant worlds, as large as the planet they rode, but millions of miles distant in Jupiter's titanic gravity field. But their light was enough to show dim alleyways and fences made of wire and some woven, fibrous stuff.

"Right, Rod. Check the control system and let it go," Penton said softly.

Five seconds later Blake was in and after a few more moments of swift examination he started from the curb. The machine started with a swift, smooth rush, and the soft whirr of the blowers and pumps was the only sound from the engine. Rapidly Blake got the feel of the apparatus, the two steering pedals, the lever that controlled its speed by increase or relaxation of pressure on the grip. Relaxed, it became a brake of fair power; squeezed, the car shot forward with amazing acceleration.

"All right. I have it now. We need lights, and I didn't figure them out. They must be in the dash control."

Penton worked swiftly over the dash with the aid of the hand flash he carried. Suddenly lights blazed on, and Blake sped on his way with more assurance.

Blake squeezed harder on the control, and the silent engine behind drove the car forward with a powerful, steady push. Rapidly, fully forty miles an hour, they cruised through the deserted district. The street that had led them straight toward their goal came to an end, and Blake hesitated at the curve, muttering at the inefficient brake system. Then he went right. Presently, on a more traveled street, he went left. More cars were about them.

As they headed toward the city, traffic became heavier, and Blake anxiously watched the system, trying to learn the rules of the road. They drove on the left, moving at a lively clip.

"They have traffic lights," said Penton quietly. "I just spotted the damn things. It's a block system, like New York's. See—way up ahead you can see that yellow light. That's stop. Red is go. We'll have to stop at this next block."

But traffic became heavier. Lights became confusing. And suddenly a bright flush crept over the sky, and almost immediately Jupiter loomed on the skyline. Five blocks later they were hopelessly caught in a traffic jam in the heart of the city. Drivers near them looked—and left. Beside them they had seen, driving a car, two monstrous, squat beings, with great ropes and bundles of inhuman muscles. To them they appeared like horrible animals incredibly become intelligent.

Blake opened his door.

"All off here. Transfer. Last stop. We can't drive through those stalled cars, and somehow I don't think the drivers are coming back." Penton got out the other side, and silently they walked up the line of traffic. Behind them doors opened hastily, and feet scuttled away. Blake crept up beside the leading car, a gleaming, seven-passenger sedan, and rose abruptly at the driver's window. He looked quietly at the occupant. A gray-haired Lanoor stared back, and slowly his eyes closed. He shook his head and opened them very wide, then beat it.

Penton climbed in first, and Blake took the late occupant's seat.

"The lights have changed," Penton said. They made nearly fifteen blocks. Then they changed cars again, taking the first car in line—and a dozen glass bubbles of sleep-gas crackled around them. Blake leapt upward, to the top of a car, and crashed through into the seat. He settled back in sleep before he could extricate himself.

Penton, who had started down the road in great leaps, looked back—and leaped faster. A two-foot thick, doughy mass was rolling of its own volition in his direction. He turned down a side street and increased his pace. He began to jump from side to side but it caught up with him.

It was soft, and squashy, but rubbery. It simply clung about his feet, and crept slowly up and over his legs, up his body, while he tore great holes in the doughiness that persistently grew together again. Desperately he drove his hand into his pocket while the Lanoor police ran toward him with their slow, exaggerated strides, gas bombs in hands. A glass bulb arched forward, but fell short of him.

Then his hand came free with the flashlight, as the crawling, doughy stuff crept about his other arm. An instant later the thing was bouncing and bounding down the street madly, from side to side, throwing itself in all directions, smashing down the rapidly approaching Lanoor, and rebounding with evident terror. Somehow the flashlight had driven it away.

Penton loped easily into an alley, and after several blocks of leaping fences, circled back. A crowd of Lanoor guardsmen were carefully roping Blake. The Earthmen lay inert in the roadway with his head thrown back, heavy snores gurgling forth. Penton walked as near as he felt was reasonably safe, and looked. An empty car stood nearby. He headed for it. It was a light roadster, and after some calculations he started it in the direction of Blake. The Lanoor guardsmen peppered it with glass bubbles; two doughy things tried to mesh its powerful wheels and were torn up, only to reform accidentally as one large one. The guardsmen scattered as the car rolled quietly forward and coasted to a stop.

Blake had already begun to stir, and Penton stopped. Evidently his previous exposure to the gas seemed to confer a semi-immunity. Methodically he released his friend. "I think," said Penton, thoughtfully, "that it is time to seek lodging for the day. This looks like a pleasantly dilapidated section."

III. THE SHLEATH

Penton looked down the shabby street. His view was restricted somewhat, because even though it was the widest of numerous sad cracks in the even sadder wreck that had once been a house and now sheltered them, it was narrow. A Lanoor was walking down the far side, stumbling through a series of dreary mud puddles in a peculiarly automatonlike way. Abruptly he halted stock still in the center of an unusually well developed puddle and shook his head slowly. It weaved about dangerously on the pipe-stem neck, and the shabbily dressed giant looked dazedly about him. After a while he started on vaguely, a gradual deepening of purpose putting increasing firmness in his gangling walk.

Penton sighed and turned away. He nodded to Blake and sat down.

"He's started. He did just what I ordered him to. Unless some Shaloor for some impossible reason picks that one man out of all the city to practice hypnotism on, those hypnotic orders I gave him are going to work, and he will bring P'holkuun here. It ought not to take more than an hour."

"But will he come? And will it do any good, if he does? He didn't help us before," protested Blake.

"He will for two reasons. The chances are the Shaloor won't know that trick about crotonaldehyde—I used something else, a catalyst that intensified the action—and they are going to be mighty mystified as to how in Nine Planets and Great Spaces we took the starch out of that wall. They'll be even more worried about the way that doughball they sicced on me backfired when I used the flashlight. He'll come, and he will probably help, now that we have shown him we can do something the Shaloor can't. I think we have an hour to wait."

They actually had less than an hour. A small roadster came slowly up the street, and stopped four or five doors away. The tall Lanoor got out. With some trepidation, evidently, he came over and cautiously opened the door.

"Come in, P'holkuun. You are a welcome sight."

"You've caused a great deal of trouble," the Lanoor greeted them. "The Shaloor have posted many guards about the palace; it has made any hope of a revolution useless for some time. They have taken the sleep-gas throwers away from the Lanoor guards, leaving them only swords. And the *shleath* are all locked up."

"Is a *shleath*," asked Penton thoughtfully, "a doughy thing without any legs, but possessed of a peculiarly unpleasant odor, and a miraculous slime?"

"No," the Lanoor sighed. "You have no idea of what *shleath* are. Those were *grethlanth* they turned on you last night. The *shleath* are fifty feet in diameter, but otherwise much like those things. The Shaloor are still very much puzzled by the way the *grethlanth* ran away from you. They are fearless, and never before have they run from a prisoner."

Penton smiled, grimly.

"That, my friend, was electricity. It was one of the forces the Shaloor have not guessed. Here, moisten your two fingers like this, and touch this little metal piece." Penton illustrated the action, and the

Lanoor hesitatingly touched the terminals of the flash. Instantly he jumped three feet backward and fell to the floor.

Slowly he sat up, shaking his head, while Penton and Blake looked at each other curiously.

"That—that is horrible! Put it away!" gasped the Lanoor. "It made all my muscles writhe into knots. It made my heart contract as though a giant had squeezed it. It is horrible!"

"It is electricity," said Penton slowly, "and you seem to be very sensitive to it, much more so than we are. Now, what did you say a *shleath* was?"

"It is a great mass of protoplasm jelly which obeys readily the will of its controller," replied P'holkuun, rubbing his arm, and eyeing the flash uneasily. "It cannot be killed, because if part is poisoned that part is split off. If it is shot or cut, that does no harm. It is not affected by sleep-gas. It is immensely strong, and can assume any form. The Shaloor conquered the Lanoor rulers originally by sending *shleath* up a small drain pipe in the form of a thread of protoplasm, and having it assume the form of a roller in the barred and defended fortress where the Lanoor rulers were. The *shleath* digest anything the Shaloor want them to. They can dissolve even metal. Only glass is impervious to them. If there is even a ventilation hole, the *shleath* can seep through."

"How many are there?"

"Thousands. They use them as work animals when need be, because they can seep under a heavy stone, girder, or mass of metal, and gradually all come under it so that the mass is lifted. Or they can hang down as a sticky cable from a high place, wrap around the stone, and contract to lift it. If an ordinary *shleath* is not strong enough, four or a hundred devour each other and form one big one, and that does the work. In the last revolt, a thousand *shleath* made a ring around the whole Lanoor army, and contracted till they were just one large lump. The army was then part of the *shleath*."

Blake looked fixedly at Penton.

"I think," he said in English, "we'd best find the shortest route for another planet. I don't like the sound of these overstuffed amoebas. But I'd love to stack them up against the Martian *thushol*. Couldn't that pair have a time?"

"We'll have to get to the ship, P'holkuun. Then we can use its power to defeat your enemies."

The Lanoor shifted his feet, and looked across the room.

"The ship," he said finally, "has been moved to the palace. Twenty *shleath* did that last night. The Shaloor knew that you would make for the ship, so they put it where they could make sure you didn't get it. They are all in the palace, and they have the ship in the inner courtyard. That is the place we call the court of the *shleath*. I do not know how you will get your ship. Maybe you could make magic on a Shaloor as you did with the strange man you sent to me. The Shaloor are working to make defenses, because they are afraid of you. They are even more afraid of the ship, so they have not touched it. If you can make a Shaloor do as the Lanoor you sent to me did, perhaps you can get the *shleath* out of the way. But no Lanoor can move them; they cannot be imprisoned; they never die."

"Can you feed them until they are groggy?"

"No, they just break up into more *shleath*, so there are twice as many and twice as hungry."

Penton looked slowly at Blake. "If you don't like the *shleath*, maybe we better decide to stay here for a while," he sighed at length. "You are sure there were not any leftover *thushol* on the ship? One of those Martian beasts might seriously distract the Shaloor just now."

"When Greek meets Greek," sighed Blake. "I'd love to see what would happen if an angry *shleath* met a Martian *thushol*. Would the *thushol* turn into an indigestible rock, or would he imitate a bigger *shleath* and eat the one that had attacked him? It is a beautiful, theosophical problem as to why the Lord ever let anything like that exist—"

"He didn't. The Shaloor invented the *shleath* and from what the Martians told us, the *thushol* invented themselves. You know, Ted, back on Mars old Loshthu told us all about the *thushol*. Rearrange the letters in his name and they practically spell *thushol*! I'll bet he really was one of them, and was laughing up his sleeve at us all the while! But that's not the point. The idea is to get inside the ship without getting inside a *shleath*." He turned to the Ganymedian. "P'holkuun, can you start the rebellion?"

"Not until you can stop the *shleath*," answered the Lanoor firmly. "The rest of my people won't even talk rebellion until they are sure they won't be used for tidbits. You have never had a fifty-foot glob of jelly scrunch down on your best friend, and watched the expression of horror fade from his face because his face was dissolving out from under the expression."

"P'holkuun, sit down a minute. I want to think," said Penton gustily, as he squatted cross-legged on the floor. "I have to find out what part of our science will beat your science. I know there is some item. Tell me things. Can you or your men get access to a metal-worker's shop? A place where there are all kinds of metals? And can you make there for me, many hundreds of small, metal machines? They will be simple, but I know a thing of science that will, I think, save you from further trouble with the *shleath*."

"We can get some metals. Not the yellow metal, or the heavy, kingly metals. Only Lanoor work in the metal shops, so we can make machines, if they are simple enough, and small enough to conceal."

"Good. Bring me, as soon as possible, a sample of all the different metals you can find. And—one of those doughy things—a *grethlanth*—that the police set on me the other night. Can you do it?"

"Yes," said P'holkuun, somewhat doubtfully. "But can you do anything?"

Penton smiled. "Friend, when I get into that sacred court of theirs, the Shaloor are going to come out of the palace faster than they have ever before moved. I shall want only about a dozen courageous Lanoor; all the rest of the rebels will stay well outside the palace and catch the Shaloor as they come out. They will come out very rapidly. And I would not advise any of your people to remain within six blocks of the palace."

"They couldn't anyway. The Shaloor live all about the palace. If you are sure—"

Blake lay down gently in the corner after P'holkuun went. He was tired. The atmosphere of the little planet was enervating. Furthermore, he only half believed in Penton, and Penton became as communicative as the surrounding walls.

* * * *

Blake slept. He slept quite peacefully until he was startled from his sleep by queer chirpings, cracklings, and loud bumpings. He sat up, only to be knocked flat by a massive, doughy affair that smacked into him, and swooshily dropped over his shoulder. Laboriously he struggled up again and looked at the dirty-gray mass that was cavorting crazily about the floor in the dim light of dusk.

Evidently P'holkuun had come and gone, and had supplied Blake with a *grethlanth*.

Penton was dashing madly about the floor picking up something, while the unspeakable dirty-whiteness was dashing about twice as madly—and abruptly dashed out of the window shrieking and gurgling unhappily.

"Well—maybe it's—all for the—best. That's hard work—here. Bending like that."

"What in the name of the Nine Wavering Worlds got into that thing?" asked Blake. "It acted as though the floor were red hot, and every time it hit it jumped higher."

"Copper," said Penton, "and magnesium. I wondered what pH value their metabolism used. Evidently it's greater than seven rather than less. But zinc does well enough, and they can get that. Copper though is expensive."

"It may make sense, but I don't see it. Where's P'holkuun?"

"Coming back now. His men were stationed outside to catch that thing when it got loose. I—here he is."

P'holkuun stuck his great head in. He looked about the very dimly lighted room.

"It went out very quickly. I thought it might have broken away and succeeded in attacking you as we had ordered it. The men have chased it two blocks now, and it is still going very rapidly. It refuses to obey at all."

"That's fine." Penton smiled. "Did it attack anyone?"

"The first one who tried to stop it. It simply rolled over him, and hastened away. What is this weapon?"

"Make me as many hundreds of these machines as you possibly can, P'holkuun, and I will take the palace with a dozen Lanoor."

Penton held out a web of wiring, a pancake of interwoven coppery and silvery wires nearly eighteen inches across. The intricate hookup of wires led into a small, solid, egg-shaped mass at the heart of the network, an ovoid of black, plastic material.

"You can make a great many, I think. And remember to make that whole device exactly as I have, changing no slightest detail, particularly as to the constitution of the central mass. Is it understood?"

"I will." P'holkuun looked somewhat wide-eyed at the savage little device that had sent the utterly fearless, nerveless defender of the Lanoorian peace scuttling out the window in such terror that it absolutely refused to obey orders.

IV. THE WHITE FLOWERS

P'holkuun halted. Ahead, the narrow corridor cut through the solid rock turned, and beyond the turn it was a passageway lined with cut stone mortared in place.

"We enter the palace soon. No Lanoor is supposed to know of this corridor, as I say, and to prevent suspicion, the Shaloor station no Lanoor guards, and do not so much as guard it themselves. But they have men watching this night beyond that wall. They are suspicious—almost know that rebellion is starting. For four days now, you have been free, and they have not heard from you, have seen no sign of your existence. They believe you have obtained help, but they have received no word of a general uprising. And"—he looked at Penton from the corner of his eyes, rather doubtfully—"they know that no dozen men can take their palace, or menace them."

"Yes. They also know that no man can stand against a *shleath*, or any save a Shaloor order him. They know a great many things. A most surprising number of those things are all wrong. Is there a door ahead?"

"Yes. Locked, with a heavy steel bolt. But—you said you could open that."

Penton smiled and nodded to Blake. Blake shifted two dozen of the flat, woven webs he carried to the dozen or so Lanoor who had accompanied them, each man rearranging the webs he already carried to take on the extra. Then the Earthman went forward.

The door was a secret panel on the other side, but from here it was obvious enough. A panel of thick, dense wood, a dark green, no doubt polished beautifully on the other side that opened into the main hall of the palace.

But from this side it was rough, and studded with locking mechanisms. Two heavy steel hinges supported it, and a series of three steel bars a half inch thick, operated by levers in the manner of a bank-vault lock, held it in place with all the rigidity of the surrounding wall. No careless hand could detect it from the far side.

Blake wrapped his fingers about the bars, braced his feet solidly, and pulled slowly, with greater and greater force. The mild steel gave under the strain, and slowly the bar backed out of the socket that held it.

Just before it was free, Blake transferred his attention to the second, and then to the third. The Lanoorians listened to his panting breath, and watched the writhing muscles in silent awe. The Earthman was to them as unnatural as a superintelligent gorilla would be to Earthmen.

Blake backed off and rested, till his heavy panting in the thin air of the little planet quieted. Finally he stood up again, and nodded.

"Ready, I guess. Now, once more, what will we have to look out for, P'holkuun?"

"They have guns, mostly air-powered guns. They are almost noiseless, there is no smoke, the source of the shot cannot be detected. But they will not shoot through heavy cloth. The explosion guns do. First they will try the sleep-gas, until they see that we are immune, thanks to your discovery that a series of five doses made a man safe. Then—the White Flowers."

"Just what are the White Flowers?" asked Penton.

P'holkuun shrugged his shoulders.

"They used it only once. They are afraid of it themselves, so they will be reluctant to try it. It is a mold that turns a healthy man into a moldering, putrescent corpse in thirty seconds. The flesh falls from his bones in white lumps. And anything that touches him, or passes near, within thirty hours—follows him! So, if you see a man turn white, and hear his scream—there is no need to help such a one. Leave him quickly. And we must go quickly now. I know the way we are to go, all my men here do. You must stay with us; if you cannot, seek the innermost court."

"Good. Go ahead, Blake," said Penton. "I'll take the lower half." Together, the two Earthmen approached the door, and took hold. The steel bars popped from their sockets with a vast droning clatter, to vibrate like plucked reeds. Immediately the two men jumped through the opened door, the Lanoorians behind them. The great central hall was bright with the glow-lights, and a half-dozen Shaloor were streaking across the room toward them, drawing their gas-guns as they came.

A shrill cry was spreading through the palace, echoing from room to room. Feet began running in unseen passages, and somewhere women's shriller voices called out. Two Lanoor servants appeared momentarily, their eyes opening in surprise at the sight, then narrowing in sudden concentration as they vanished into familiar passages.

Blake's arm flung back. A rounded, nicely weighted stone flew from it with the super Lanoorian force a Terrestrial could give it. An attacking Shaloor doubled with a howl of pain and an instant later another fell with a little groan, the side of his head crushed in. Gas bombs fell about them as P'holkuun led the way to a branching, wood-paneled corridor on the far side of the room.

"They will concentrate to defend the inner court, since it is known that you have come," P'holkuun called back. "Hurry."

A pair of Lanoorians had spread out behind them, and their swords were flashing in efficient butchery. The Shaloor were vanishing now, into the various rabbit-warren passages.

P'holkuun led them at a sharp run down the passage, past a dozen intersecting warrens and into a smaller passage.

"P'holkuun!" a strange low voice warned softly. "Not that way, the gates will close. Turn aside. The third—right." Feet vanished. P'holkuun halted in indecision.

"I wonder if that was a Shaloor?" he asked unhappily.

"It was my cousin!" exclaimed one of the Lanoor. "He is a secretary—"

They took the third to the right.

"But I am lost now," P'holkuun muttered. "I do not know this route. Why didn't he join us to help—"

From a room on one side a Lanoor stepped out.

"You'd probably have shot me by mistake. Come." The man had two of the air guns, and a blood-stained sword. "They are gathered to defend the great inner court. They have closed all entrances with steel grills, save the one that they want you to take, the *S'logth* gate. That is open—open for the *shleath*. What do you hope to do?"

"Lead us there." Penton smiled. "The sooner we reach the *shleath*, the better. What weapons have they?"

The Lanoor shifted his slight weight to his right foot.

"Some strange things they found on the ship of the strangers. A little thing, like a pistol, or sleep-gas thrower. But it throws nothing, only light, and not bright light at that. A Shaloor died handling it, and they made two Lanoor find out the secret. Now they have twenty. There is another thing they will use if they must, but they fear it, for none of us have been able to make it work without terrific explosions. But the explosions destroy what they hit, so they may use it even so."

"Damn," said Penton softly. "They can stop the *shleath* with the ultra-violet pistols. And the atomic bullet guns. They might go so far as to attack the ship with them. Not even the ship could stand one of those atomic bullets. Thank God they're still more afraid of them than we are. All we can do is try. They won't know just what they are doing, and we may still get away with it."

"Lead the way, man."

Again they started, through more devious, involved passages than they had taken before. Through rooms where Lanoor servants looked, saw them, and looked blindly away, through rooms where startled Lanoor women rose angrily from sleep, and quieted with a grim smile as they saw who invaded their rooms. Down narrow corridors, through smoking kitchens. Down a long corridor—

"No, I tell you, no!" a Lanoor's voice shouted in exasperation. "They have not come this way. Why should they? They will go some other way if they have a particle of sense, and they will go entirely away if they know what I know." And then came the angry curses of a Shaloor. Abruptly they dived into a side lane, and P'holkuun grinned.

"The Shaloor cannot hear well. Nor see, for all of that. But the Lanoor hear us."

"P'holkuun! Who—ah, it is you," the Lanoor's voice continued. "They are waiting for you at the gate now with three *shleath* in hiding. Go back. You must try at some other time. The city has heard, and it is roaring with rebellion. The Shaloor are preparing to bring out the *shleath* as the crowd grows outside the palace. But go back. They are ready for you, and they have a new weapon."

P'holkuun looked at the new Lanoor recruit uneasily.

"Did you hear that, Earthman?" he asked Penton.

"Did you hear of the new weapon, Lanoor?" returned Penton. "Do you think they will ever know less than they know now? Be less ready to meet you with strange weapons? Do you think you can ever have a better chance than with the men who invented the weapons you fear? And know more about them than all the Shaloor on the planet? If ever in time you have had a breath of hope, you have it now. Come on before that breath expires." Penton started on down the corridor. "And you don't have to worry about the *shleath*. They will be more worry to the Shaloor than to you."

"Then stop. That is the door that leads to the hall of the *S'logth* gate. If you open the door, the *shleath* will be in here at once."

"What is out there, then?" Blake demanded.

"There are, apparently, three *shleath*, and the Lord of Worlds only knows how many Shaloor, waiting to shoot, gas, bomb, and kill us in every other conceivable way."

"Where are the Shaloor?"

"They will be in the high gallery. The *S'logth* gate goes up three stories, but we are on the first, since only thus can one enter the inner courtyard. They will be on the second and third galleries, and they will be watching for us. We cannot enter here until, somehow, the Shaloor are driven out."

"How do we get to the third floor gallery, then?"

P'holkuun looked to the Lanoor secretary who had joined them, Tathuol. The man shook his head.

"I can try. But it will do little good, since there we will be unable to reach and enter the gate we should pass through, because we can't reach the floor. And the Shaloor may have the steel grills in the way."

"If I once get my hands on one of the weapons they stole from our ship," said Blake grimly, "all the Shaloor on the planet, and all the *shleath*, steel grills, stone walls and assorted animals and plants won't stop me. Just get me near one of those Shaloor."

The way was a winding, climbing corridor, and it led them through back rooms and twisting flights of stairs. It led them up trap-doors in closets, and in impossible ways. Finally Tathuol halted.

"That is the door. There will be half a hundred Shaloor waiting for us out there."

"Don't disappoint them, then. Come on!" Penton yanked open the door, and jumped out, low. Fully the promised fifty Shaloor turned toward him, raising their guns. Instantly the walls were peppered with shot, and, with a queer hissing, droning hum, a beam of pale, deepest violet stabbed through the air. Not toward Penton, but across the great hallway to a hanging balcony on the far side! Someone howled in agony there, and together, Blake and Penton charged down the hundred foot length of the balcony.

It was only some twenty feet wide, and between them, with P'holkuun in effective action, the balcony was cleared in less than fifteen seconds. Cleared, for the Shaloor jerked and moved on the courtyard floor, eighty feet below.

Penton stared about him. Across the courtyard, four similar balconies hung at the same level, and four more below. On his right, on this same side, another balcony clung to the dark stone wall, and two more on the left. Four below him. The great ceiling arched low above his head, studded with hundreds of glowing lights. And in the great hall below, three monstrous things pulsed and staggered, three things like green, gold and purple amoebas fifty feet in diameter.

They were surging and wavering madly, and then suddenly they stopped and ran together. Horribly they merged into a single, frightful mass of pulsing, nauseous flesh. An oozing, angry mass of protoplasm, it charged for the wall, and miraculously sent a vast finger of jelly-stuff sprouting swiftly upward, past the balcony, toward them!

Abruptly, Penton heard the clanking sounds of dropped metal, soft moans of terror, and scampering feet. The Lanoor were leaving. Only P'holkuun and a half-dozen others stood, white-faced, beside the Earthmen. "The *shleath*—coming—" said P'holkuun stiffly.

Penton crouched. The wall of the balcony, some four feet high, was carved with an intricate design of flowers and trees, and intricate spaces cut through the stone. There was an angry silence in the court. Only the soft, horrible *shluffing*, slobbering sounds of that vast monstrosity climbing the wall. It had dwindled to a twenty-foot thing of green jelly with a purple, angry bruiselike knot in its middle, with golden thread shot through it. But up the stone wall, to within a few feet of the balcony, the questing mustard-green, pseudopodal arm clung tenaciously to the minute grips it found. Penton crouched and waited, peering through the tiny holes.

"Pick up three of those webs, Blake," said Penton, softly. "And wait until that thing reaches up here."

Somehow P'holkuun made himself move. He handed Penton a half-dozen of the flimsy, interwoven webs of silver and copper wires. They looked like metal spider webs with black, rubbery spiders clumped at their centers.

Then the vast arm reached up to the balcony. Thick fingers of slime reached through the openings of the balcony wall, and waved with a horrible suggestion of individual, hateful life. The great, green wave curled smoothly over the wall, and sprouted thick tentacles that stabbed out toward the Earthman as he rose. In his hand the flash, with its projecting, copper terminals, blackened by the burning arc that had fused the lock, gleamed dimly.

He thrust his hand toward one of those jelly-ropes, and braced as the thing clamped viciously about him. Then he pressed the button that shot fifty volts of powerful current into the vast mass of protoplasm.

Somehow it screamed. The city quieted to that ineffable shriek. An unspeakable hatred was in it, and an indescribable terror. The rope turned livid yellow, and contracted so swiftly that the mass on the floor jerked halfway up the wall to meet it, and fell with a liquid splashing plop. The mass heaved; it split into three separate pieces, then half a dozen, and they all howled.

Accurately, Penton tossed one of the metal webs so that it fell onto the center of one of the pulsing, writhing things on the floor. The *shleath* shrieked with the same unspeakable, evil hatred, and the same awful terror, but somehow it whined; it begged. It scuttled into a corner and cowered there.

And another one of the blind, terror-stricken things touched the spider of black, and gold, and silver. It leaped five feet into the air, and splintered on the floor. The great *shleath* split into a hundred tiny things that rolled and scuttled and bounded with little evil squeaks of terror as they accidentally touched the black spider.

The larger ones were coming under control. Reluctantly, angrily they moved about, incorporating the smaller ones into their vast bulks. They joined again to two vast masses that charged for the wall. Penton dropped another of the webs. Then, in swift succession, two more.

There was point to their anger now. They howled, but they howled with directed anger. From the horribly stinging balcony they turned to the masters that drove them on. A wave of slime engulfed the lower balcony directly below the Earthmen. Penton watched the struggling Shaloor turn horribly red as their mouths gaped open in the thick, transparent jelly. They turned red, and stained the green about them, and struggled jerkily, then feebly; and through the clouding redness that grew in the green jelly, vague, shadowy things that might have been white bone here, or bared vital organs there, began to show.

Penton turned away. The *shleath* was stretching out an arm toward the nearby balcony below, where milling Shaloor shot hissing pistols at it, and finally—something white blossomed in the greenness. The *shleath* seemed to suck in the whiteness and engulf it, but the white splotch grew, and spread with an awesome rapidity. The *shleath* writhed and spewed out the mass of white and green life stuff. Then the rope looped out again.

Softly violet, softly humming, the beam of one of the stolen pistols stabbed from the balcony. It struck the courtyard below, and wandered wildly, erratically about while the wave of green washed over the balcony. Again a white splotch blossomed, and again. Twice the thing spit them forth with masses of its own stuff. Then the white blossomed on an infected Shaloor, and he fell screaming, tearing at his leg, as the stuff whirled through his veins. He writhed over the edge of the balcony, and lay beside the white tufts of ejected tissue from the *shleath*, white as they, and growing soft and downy.

V. BIFOCAL VISION

Abruptly the wildly wavering beam of the UV pistol snapped out. Tensely Penton watched as a pseudopod of the *shleath* lapped up a Shaloor. The one with the stolen weapon seemed to be concentrating, his brows wrinkled in fear-filled thought. With both hands, he held the pistol, and abruptly swept it around the *shleath*. It exploded into flare, and the *shleath* howled in agony again. Dense, nauseous smoke welled up from the flaring spot where the ultra-violet beam tore into it, bubbling horribly. The thing dropped from the balcony, splitting into a hundred parts as it fell.

Blake spoke softly.

"I've been usefully engaged. There are about fifty less Shaloor. They have been too busy to watch, and these guns work. There was only one UV pistol here, and that went over the edge with one of the Shaloor."

"P'holkuun, you said they couldn't see?" Penton asked softly. "What do you mean?"

"They can see. But they don't point right. They never drive, they never fly planes. They seldom write, or do experiments themselves. We do not understand fully. But there is something the matter with their eyes."

"Thank God for that," said Penton. "I think I know what it is. They've joined the two halves of the brain, and are far more brilliant than any creature has a right to be, but they pay for it. Only one half the brain does all the thinking. That's true enough. But both halves see, and both halves hear. Both halves help with moving the body about. Somehow, when they cross those two halves of the brain for greater keenness, they see double. They probably hear double, too. They can't coordinate arm and eye well. They forced themselves to learn to move a bit, but they can't make themselves see straight.

"They are more intelligent, no doubt of that, for they have more UV guns than we made. They figured out that unknown system to that extent in one week's time. But they not only see double, but by some psychological trick, they see the wrong image best! They missed us when we appeared suddenly. That Shaloor that tried to kill the *shleath* with the UV gun shot up all the court but for the spot where the creature was. They can't move quickly, and they can't see straight. That gives us a far better chance, and changes my plans a bit. P'holkuun, can we get somewhere where we can throw the webs into the inner court? Let's finish the job."

Tathuol nodded.

"Yes. Come." He led them back, through twisting corridors, through rooms where terrified Lanoor whispered and asked questions. They had heard the screams of the maddened *shleath*. The news was spreading. Then they reached a barred gate, a grillwork of locked bars that closed off the corridor. Beyond it they looked into a great courtyard a quarter of a mile across. The vast ramifications of the palace surrounded it on every side. And in it half a hundred of the giant *shleath* wavered and stirred uneasily, crowding down at the gate beyond which they had heard the strange shrieks of their fellows.

Somehow those giant masses of jelly had a brain and understanding. And they were restless. The glow-lamps cast only dim sparkles of light on hulking masses of greenish jelly. And, out in the middle of the court, silver metal on the *Ion*, the ship that had brought Penton and Blake to this world, glistened faintly.

"Oh, for the wings of an angel! How in blazes are we going to get there?" Blake mourned.

Penton began tossing the black and silver and gold of the spiders methodically through the bars. One—five—a dozen. Some fell short, some long of their mark. It was hard to aim at an angle on a light world of unfamiliar gravity. Then two in quick succession landed.

"Back—back to the entranceway where we can get into the courtyard," Penton yelled over the shrieks of the two monsters. A giant began stamping. The whole palace shook to the thud of his tread. Then it stopped. Human feet began running somewhere, and the shouts of the Shaloor pierced the roaring that came from the inner court. Penton hesitated. Then he gathered all the spider webs, and threw them into the yard below, spinning them all over the court. Dozens of them skimmered into the night to fall with soft, clinking rustles. Three times he scored hits. But now restless, wandering *shleath* were accidentally touching the stinging electric traps.

The radiating copper and zinc wires reaching out from the rubber egg at the center were charged by the little battery protected in the black, elastic shell. The first electric batteries on this world! And these *shleath*, the mighty, indestructible *shleath* howled in malignant terror. They had no true skin, they were vast masses of naked, unprotected protoplasm. Each touch of those charged wires sent a minute electric current charging through their vast masses—torturing, unbearable current.

It was happening there in the courtyard as Penton had known it would. The vast yard was boiling with the protoplasmic Titans, their weird, gold-shot bulks glistening in the dim lights, their weird, anguished cries shrilling in the night. Outside the palace a vast echo was rolling back, the vast angry roar of the aroused Lanoor rebels. Here below, as the elephantine bulks of the restlessly moving *shleath* touched one of the electrically charged webs, the shocking current made it writhe and heave. Frantically they sought escape, escape that was barred by the glass walls, by the special doors.

Shaloor were appearing at the lower gates, ordering them, directing them. Abruptly a mighty, shining bulk rolled down to the pompous midget, and whipped him into extinction with its glistening pseudopod. And the Thing howled. A shock-disc touched it. Every move of its sprawled bulk touched one of the scattered shock-discs. From other gratings about the great court P'holkuun's reinforcements were tossing in the webs now; the court was paved with them.

The *shleath* found only one escape. They were dividing now, splitting and dwindling, splitting till their jellied bulks covered more, but smaller areas. Smaller, smaller they became as more and more of the webs fell. They could slip between them now, find some surcease from the unknown horror of electric currents whose tiniest trickle made them writhe in agony.

Penton watched in silence. The fifty, and seventy-five-foot Titans had dwindled, screaming. None was larger than a two-foot globe of jelly!

"Put on those boots," said Penton softly, "and come on." From his waist, he himself unstrapped the network of charged wires, and wrapped them about his legs. From his belt two sets of wires dangled, connecting the leggings to five tiny cells. "Now, P'holkuun, where is the man with the rope? We can go down there now, if we can open this grill. No *shleath* will dare to touch us now. This grill is bolted in two places, and I think the atomic flash has still power enough to burn two."

The atomic flashlight was changed now; two heavy copper leads had been soldered to its terminals. As they touched the steel bolts, the hissing green flame of the copper arc shrilled into the metal, twice. The flash tube, its storage device of twisted atoms intended only for the light task of providing illumination, hummed and grew warm. The bolt sputtered suddenly and fell molten. The lurid green flare ate at another bar.

It glowed red, then white—and parted. Another—and Penton dropped the flash tube with a curse. It glowed for a moment, and died, its last dregs of energy exhausted. Together the Earthmen heaved at the weakened grill. The grating moved a fraction of an inch protestingly, and held. Again and again the two men heaved; finally all the Lanoor who could reach it added their strength.

Then, from a distant grating, a violet beam of death reached out, and crackled the stone twenty feet from them.

Penton ran. "Damn," he groaned. "They've spotted that grating, and they won't let us near it now. We've got to try some other way. I wonder—"

He started down the corridor, turned back to the next grating, and tried it. It was locked as solidly.

"Tathuol, can you lead me to a grating where there are some Shaloor posted, at least one of whom has one of our weapons?"

The Lanoor thought a moment. "I can lead you to the one from which they fired just a while ago."

"Good. P'holkuun, if you have a brave man, tell him to stay at that grate we left, and test it every few minutes until we give him the signal to stop. He has to keep out of the way of the beam, but he has to keep the man who is running it interested. Anybody want the job?"

P'holkuun laughed mirthlessly.

"I doubt it. Go ahead, I will take care of it. If my luck is bad, remember your promise to free my people."

"Right, my friend." Penton nodded slowly. "They will be, before the sun rises. But—be spry." Penton took the Lanoor's hand in a firm grasp for a moment, then followed Tathuol. Through the rabbit-warren palace they dodged. Once they met a searching party of half a dozen Shaloor armed with the little yellow tubes that carried the deadly White Flower—and had kept out of sight. But Tathuol knew the maze-like routes of the building far better than did those lords by proxy, for their strange, crossed vision made walking difficult, and they hated it.

"Beyond that turn," the Lanoor said at last, "is the grating we saw the Shaloor fire from. I cannot guarantee that he is still there."

"Let us just hope so, then. We—ah, he is." A brief, soft glare of violet shot out from the corridor's end. Noiselessly Penton rounded the corner, Blake close behind him. Four Shaloor stood watching, looking out across the courtyard to a distant gateway where metal bars shone dully red. Cracked, blistered stone told of the violence of the pistol they used.

"He is trying to get us to melt that gate away," said one of the Sha-loor uneasily.

"Much good may it do him. I'll get him the next time he shows, because I haven't changed the direction since the last shot. I—"

Penton's powerful arms wrapped two of the bean-stalk giants while Blake caught the others. Instantly six of the Lanoor who had followed them descended and in the space of seconds, the Shaloor glared in anger from their bonds.

* * * *

Penton examined the gun he held.

"It's one of ours. Needs a new charge, too; not more than ten sec-ond's life left. This one is set for steel, too, and we haven't any. Well—"

With a knife for a screwdriver, and two bits of metal in pinching fingers for a wrench, Penton opened the butt of the weapon, and pulled out the tiny reel that carried the iron-wire fuel. Then he adjusted four tiny screws and tore a strip of the copper wire from his protective leg-gings. With Blake's aid he stretched it cautiously. It was good copper, and it fined down several gauges before it broke. Then he inserted that into the reel, and clamped the gun together.

"Now, if my memory is good, and I have the right constants for the slow release of the copper's energy, we'll get out in fine style. And if it isn't—we'll go out in fine style," he added grimly.

Penton aimed the gun at the grate, and pulled the trigger. Instantly the beam shot forth, a blazing inferno of light that volatilized the grat-ing almost instantly, speared through to the courtyard below, and sent up bubbling smoke. The squealing anger of the *shleath* changed to a vast shrieking. Penton hurled the weapon to the floor. Slowly a glow built up in it, a glow that spread from the tip of the barrel to the breech, and the smoke of the wiring rose from it.

Blake and Penton were two hundred feet down the corridor when the incredible sharpness of the explosion wave hurled them along for twenty feet, like peas from a peashooter. The clatter of falling masonry grumbled behind them, and even the steady wail of the *shleath* quieted momentarily.

Penton picked himself up gingerly.

"Not bad," he said judicially, "not perfect, but not bad. It might have been, to put it mildly, somewhat worse. We're lucky the town's still here."

Over tumbled blocks of stone that made a perfect ladder, the two men scrambled down to the courtyard. Undamaged, the *Ion* lay some fifty feet from the end of the slide that had crumbled half one wall of the yard.

It was not a path of roses. The Shaloor were on the job, and only their incredibly confused eyesight made it possible. Consistently, half the beams and bullets tore into the enraged *shleath* behind them, and half spattered before them. None came near them.

Ten feet from the entrance Penton gasped, and fell. His unprotected hand was grabbed instantly by a *shleath*, before Blake could lift him to his feet again. The touch of Blake's boot drove it away as Penton spoke: "They have the range. Get in that ship, you fool—they got my leg with a bullet."

"Uh-huh," said Blake. "You talk funny. Hold on. Even on a light world you are heavy—"

From a height of some five hundred feet, Blake looked down. Then he turned on the spotlight, and looked at the courtyard below. He adjusted some controls, and when the spotlight exactly covered that yard, he pulled a small tumbler. The light turned violet, and the heaving, greenish floor turned brown and became quiescent. The light went out. Blake pulled the microphone near him, and spoke softly, words that roared from the loudspeaker in the outer skin of the ship.

"P'holkuun, if you will come up alone in a plane tomorrow at dawn, we'll meet you. I could take that palace apart, but most of the inhabitants seem to be your folk. In the meantime, I have to pull a bullet out of Penton's leg. Tomorrow at dawn, in a plane from the local port."

THE IMMORTALITY SEEKERS

I. THE SECOND METAL

Ted Penton, of the team of Penton and Blake, regarded his companion, Rod Blake, and grinned. In the great audience hall below, twelve hundred of Callisto's scientists were assembling to hear the message of the visitors from space.

"Plenty has happened to us since Earth kicked us out for taking off some of the three hundred square miles of territory spang in the center of Europe in an atomic explosion. It's their own fault if they can't find us—outlawing research on atomic power. It was obvious when we developed atomic power that we'd be the first men to reach the other planets. And nobody can follow to bring us back unless they accepted the hated atomic power and used it."

"One," interrupted Rod Blake, ticking it off on his finger. "I learned the Martian language under the able, if painful, hypnotic teaching of a Martian master, old Loshthu. Two,"—a second finger—"I learned the Lanoor language on Ganymede by *your* hypnotic teaching. *You* are not a master of Martian telepathy, and it was more racking. Three, we are now on Callisto and I may be blowed to the nine planets and twenty-odd moons of the Solar System before I let you teach me this language that way.

"Look at the scraps we've picked up for ourselves so far: an hour after we landed on Mars we were trying desperately to get away from Mars and their damned inhabitants, the *thushol*. Then we went to Ganymede, battled their glorious *shleath* and Lanoor, and got evicted. I won't go through that headache I always collect from learning a language via your hypnotism system if we are going to be here on Callisto a year or so. I can pick up the language normally in that time; so no hypnotism. Got it?"

Penton smiled beatifically.

"The Callistans will want a speech from you at that conference that is so swiftly assembling. Just because we've had bad luck on those last two trips—"

"If you think those Lanoor that were chasing us meant no more than bad luck when we left Ganymede, why did you exhibit such surprising speed? Me, with two sound legs, and I had all that I could do to keep up with a wounded one. They weren't wishing us bad luck; they were wishing to elongate the vertebrae connecting my cranium with the rest of me, or I'm badly mistaken. Very peevish about it, too."

"H-m-m, mildly so. But then, you must admit those *shleath* were enough to make anyone peevish," Penton pointed out judicially.

"No fault of ours, We were asked to overthrow the Shaloor overlords, which we did. They should have had sense enough to keep those fifty-foot amoebas in check after that. I'd have suggested turning that courtyard where they were into a sulphuric acid swimming pool, myself."

"No fault of ours, perhaps, but they wanted someone to blame, and we were handy. If the *shleath* had had the decency to stay fifty-foot size something could be done. But now they are peeping their particularly unpleasant slime out of every rat-hole, crack and crevice in the whole city. Personally, I don't see what the Lanoor are going to do about it. The only cure I could see was to burn down the whole city—ray it out of existence. The damned things can go anywhere, through the tiniest crack; worst of all, no animal can fight them, they just digest it."

Blake was staring down through the ornamental grille that separated their room from the great audience hall below. It was almost filled up.

"By the way, Penton, what are you going to tell that Callistan assembly?"

"Various things," Penton sighed. "I'll have to figure it out as I go along. I had a chance to talk with Tha Lagth, the old commander who brought us here, for only about five minutes. They have automobiles—we rode in one; wing-flapping, flying machines—we watched them as we came down in our spaceship. But what else they have, I can't make out. I know they don't have fire, since no normal fuel will burn in this atmosphere, so I brought some things to amuse them." Penton pulled some loose, metal scraps from a pouch he wore, and a small bottle filled with sticks of yellowish wax and a watery liquid.

"White phosphorous for one," guessed Blake, "but the metal has me stopped. Oh—magnesium. Yes, that would burn anywhere."

"Some of them may have seen a flame in a laboratory, under special lab conditions, but I don't think they saw any in open air. They do have ships—we saw them in the harbor down there—can see them now for that matter. Say, they must all be motor ships, but I wonder what kind of motors they use? This air wouldn't let even a Diesel engine run. Electric—but how do they generate power?

"Anyway, that's the trouble. I want to find out what they know before I go spreading all my cards. Somehow, we have to stay here long enough to get a stock of edible food. I wish we hadn't been so bright, moving all the stuff from the ship into that apartment our friend P'holkuun gave us back on Ganymede."

"Yes," Blake said ironically, "oh Ambassador Plenipotentiary of Earth. How in the name of the wavering worlds will you support *that* claim?"

"Well"—his friend grinned—"Earth gave us a royal sendoff the last time we visited—all the big guns firing in our honor."

"Probably it was an accident they left the shells in when they fired 'em," Blake grunted. "I suppose you are playing on the fact that they can't check up on you?"

"But more immediately important, how about these Callistans? You swore up and down that they were an honest, gentlemanly race. But how sure are you?"

Penton nodded toward the closet on one side of the room, where the shimmery bulk of his spacesuit hung.

"I discarded that suit. They don't understand mental telepathy any more than we did before the Martians gave us practical lessons—even if unpleasant ones. They can't mask their thoughts, therefore, and I know what sort of ideas old Tha Lagth had while meeting us and bringing us here. He's a nice, old fellow, and all that brusque, efficient, military air of his was due to the fact that he was half scared of doing the wrong thing.

"What is the proper formula for greeting the first ambassador of an alien planet? Who should attend to it? Using uncommon good sense, the old fellow figured visitors from a foreign world called for the whole constellation of scientists instead of politicians. More power to him. The premier will undoubtedly horn in, but I thank Tha Lagth for his kindly thoughts."

"I don't mind your discarding the spacesuits," Blake objected, "half so much as I regret that the only holsters we had for the UV guns and the disintegrator pistols were part of the spacesuits. I just like that nice, rhythmic, bump-bump-bump of a dis gun when I am on planets unknown. It makes me feel very much as though I really owned the place. Which isn't so far from the truth when you have one of those ray guns on tap."

Penton shrugged.

"A dis gun puts that potential ownership in the realm of academic questions. If you have to prove it, there is nothing but dust left to own when you reach the Q.E.D. stage. Anyway, prepare to meet the assembled bright-lights of the Callistans intellectual world. Here comes Tha Lagth."

Blake turned with a sigh.

"I'm glad you'll have to do all the talking as Earth's ambassador. But look, can't you do that thought-projecting stunt so I can follow, even if—"

"Even if you won't take the trouble to learn the language?" Penton grinned. "I suppose I'll have to."

"Welcome, Tha Lagth," said Penton, smoothly shifting into Callistan. "The scientists are assembled?"

"Yes, Earthmen. If you are ready—" The old warrior looked at them with friendly dignity.

* * * *

Seated before that audience of twelve hundred Callistans, they found Penton's guess confirmed. The premier was an unusually tall man, even among the eight-foot Callistans, with gray-white hair and a jet-black beard clipped in a style strongly reminiscent of the ancient Assyrian custom.

He was pointing out the immense importance of this occasion— historic moment—two world's civilizations—the benefits of both. The director of the Sharl Technical University rose and explained the historic moment—two world's sciences—the benefits of both, Starn Druth, the most eminent scientist of Callisto, walked slowly up to the platform, an old, shaky man, his skin wrinkled with advanced age. But his speech was sharp, clever, and avoided the obvious. Penton listened with interest, and realized that the old body carried a keen, youthful mind.

Starn Druth remarked that inevitably the available supplies of chemical elements on two worlds would differ in important, perhaps vital, ways.

"There is," he pointed out, "an element which theory has shown to be of immense importance. It exists in small quantities in the sun, but has never been found here, to our regret. Our planet is light, and has lost nearly all the hydrogen, the helium and the other light atoms it originally had when the worlds cooled from creation. The heavier worlds may well have retained these elements in small but available quantities. This—"

At the back of the huge hall, a man stumbled in, a man in the green-blue uniform of the Air Force. He was panting for breath, wildly excited. Despite the efforts of the attendants who rose to stop him, he ran down the aisle shouting.

Tha Lagth rose to his feet and stepped forward sharply.

"Halt!" he roared. "What is the reason for this intrusion?"

"Commander—Commander—the ship. Their ship is made of the Second Metal!"

With a single, mighty roar, the assembly came to its feet Tha Lagth stopped abruptly, and looked to old Starn Druth. The scientist stared in sudden triumph at his colleagues.

"I said it! The heavy world retained the Second Metal!" But no one heard his voice in the clamorous shouting. Tha Lagth had taken up the gavel, and was pounding vigorously at the resonator on his desk. Slowly its sharp, piercing note struck out through the babble to quiet the hundreds of Callistans. Gradually they relaxed in their seats.

"Now, messenger," said Tha Lagth at length, "what was found?"

"A micro-sample was scraped from the hull of the stranger's ship, and analysis performed. The chief components detected were copper, cobalt, aluminum and magnesium. The bulk of the material definitely did not answer to any known test. The analysts took a second specimen and made spectroscopic tests. The scientists reported that it was definitely identified as the Second Metal. Eighty percent of the metal of the ship's hull—hundreds of tons—is the nonexistent metal!"

Starn Druth muttered something under his breath, his bright old eyes fixed on Tha Lagth. Then he spoke.

"I suggest that I explain to these strangers the importance of this Second Metal to us." He looked toward Penton eagerly.

"Most of our industry and science has been based on the study of life, bio-chemistry. Within recent years, we have learned to synthesize life-forms from inorganic elements; we make living cells, and design them for certain functions. Gradually we have developed many different types of synthetic life-forms that supply us with food, and do our work.

"But by theoretical calculations it has been shown that the greatest triumph of all, intelligent micro-life, can be produced in only one way; we know the needed combinations of elements, of amino acids and carbohydrates. Many times we have gathered these things and put them together in the proper way, but the stimulating spark has not appeared. We lack the one thing which will start that life working.

"The lower forms of life we have used have been stirred from inorganic immobility to life by the flashing of the rays of radium. To procure more intelligent forms, even more powerful rays are needed, and some of our best results have been attained by the aid of immense X-ray tubes operating at nearly ten million volts. But to create the ultimate ideal, intelligent, obedient, microscopic life, we must have rays emanating from a fifteen billion volt source! Rays of a particular type.

"Our atomic theorists have proven that in all Universe, only one thing can supply just that ray; the disintegration of the atoms of the Second Metal."

Penton nodded slowly. "Huh. Beryllium. And we made the ship out of that. It's such a light element it probably all boiled away while your planet was cooling. It's enormously rare, even on Earth."

"We need it," Starn Druth explained softly, "because with intelligent, obedient life-forms of microscopic size, we can become immortal."

Penton started. "Immortality—how?"

"By directing those life-forms to make the repairs our bodies need, by ordering them to destroy malignant growths, by injecting billions of obedient defenders when infection threatens. Our bodies naturally have certain forms of defending cells, but they act instinctively. Malignant tumors—cancer—they do not attack, because that is a growth of the body they defend. No instinct warns them. We cannot summon them to the attack when infection begins but must wait until their sluggish instinct at last warns them. With the synthetic life we know how to make, we can guarantee ourselves immunity to all disease, injury, or senile decline."

Penton looked at Starn Druth thoughtfully a moment. His racing thoughts sized up a situation that was rapidly becoming more than warm; the only beryllium on the planet was their ship. Penton and Blake were not wanted back on Earth, where further beryllium could be obtained.

It might be two years before their friends on Earth finally succeeded in convincing the government of Earth that the outlawed and vastly feared atomic motor would not blow up to destroy the planet—

"There are scattered, minute amounts of beryllium on Earth. In return for the knowledge of your technique of creating these intelligent forms of micro-life, I am sure that Earth can supply you with sufficient beryllium within one year."

Starn Druth looked toward him quizzically.

"We need beryllium within one month. Your ship could make the round trip very readily in that time."

"But beryllium is excessively rare—you know that. So finely scattered among so much rock—"

A scientist rose haltingly from the floor of the assembly. "The beryllium atom, according to our calculations," he said, "would not blend in with ordinary rocks. Even when very rare, it should occur in small, but concentrated deposits. It is insoluble, and hence would not disperse."

Penton looked at him unhappily. Callistan science was most unfortunately advanced; the man was 100 percent right. "The ore is so rare," lied Penton, "that some of our most precious jewels are made of it. Emeralds—sapphires. It was only because the metal has the property of stopping certain rays in space that we were forced to use the extremely expensive material—" Penton suggested hopefully.

It didn't go over. They might never have seen the metal, but they evidently knew plenty about its properties.

"Diamond is a rare form of a common element; certain of our jewels are a rare crystalline of aluminum oxide, a common material," said Starn Druth uneasily. "Beryllium is opaque to no known radiation, save ordinary light. What are these space-rays?" He looked toward Penton with an evident feeling that something was being concealed.

"If we return at once," said Penton finally, "I can assure you a sufficient supply, a ton or more, of beryllium within one year of my planet."

"If we use the metal of your spaceship," suggested Starn Druth softly, "we could arrange to have certain of the intelligent micro-life cells made to suit your body-chemistry. Both of you would be assured immortality. There would be much for you to learn here, and eventually we could duplicate your ship."

II. IMPERMANENT RESIDENCE

"That," explained Penton ironically, nodding toward the four, eight-foot Callistans pacing the corridors from their room, "is a guard of honor. By no means let it be thought that they are warders of our confinement."

Blake looked at them morosely. "Shut up! This is one world we haven't been kicked out of yet. And is our ship guarded! Tha Lagth ordered only four rows of guards to surround it, while the scientists worked out refining methods. I wish they had put us back in that room where we first were. Our spacesuits are there."

"Man, those Callistans have heads on them. They knew more about a metal they had never seen than I, who had built a ship of it. There was not a chance that they would forget and put us in with those suits again."

"When does it get dark here?" asked Blake suddenly. "From the looks of those shadows on the orange lawn out there, the sun hasn't moved an inch since we arrived here six hours ago."

"An inch, maybe. But not much more," Penton sighed. "This satellite always faces Jupiter with the same side, like Luna facing Earth. It takes sixteen days to go around, so it will be sixteen days before that blasted sun sets. No chance of waiting for night."

"Sixteen days? It wasn't dawn when we landed," Blake protested.

"Oh, bother, you figure it out. I count on my fingers and when I have rheumatism I make mistakes," Penton growled. "Man, next time when somebody wants something I say, 'Yes, sir. Right away, sir. You want the sun on your front steps? Oh, certainly. Just a moment.' I might have known that they wouldn't be in the mood for waiting. Reasonable enough. Old Starn Druth doesn't consider it advisable to wait a year or so while we get beryllium, and six months while they make and test that life-cell.

"Their president is just as old, and naturally most of the people that run the place are getting old, so it's not really remarkable that they want that beryllium in a hurry. If they can hold off for six months they live centuries more. If they die within that time—they lose immortality!"

"Somehow you don't seem interested in their offer of immortality yourself."

Penton looked at his friend.

"Do you think that anybody can figure out the entire life chemistry of a foreign life-form in a year, or ten years? They've studied their own for centuries, and now they don't know enough to control it, without invoking trick life-forms. They don't know their own chemistry, and with no experimental animals to work on, they wouldn't know ours in less time than it took them to learn their own. They know damn well we are here to stay, because they can't do large-scale metal work. I learned that from Starn Druth while he was thinking the problem over. All their major works are stone or wood, or plastics like bakelite.

"No fire except in laboratory lots; their electricity is derived from some sort of primary battery, since they don't have fires or steam engines, and their gravity is too light for hydro power in quantity. It'd take them fifty years, under our direction, to build up a smelting and refining industry even based on atomic power. They'd have to start from scratch."

"I have an overwhelming desire to go home," Blake commented. "How are we going to do it, though?"

"There is no use waiting for night. They have their guards planted, but not thoroughly worked out yet, so I've sort of an idea that if we just bounce out faster than they put us in, we'll catch them unprepared. Also, if we wait a few days here, there won't be enough of our ship left to worry about. Did you get the layout of the city?"

"Yes. It's a harbor city on an inland sea, more of a huge salt lake. The harbor is something like San Francisco on a miniature scale. Shaped like a Greek capital omega. We're on the left headland, in the governmental buildings, surrounded by nice, broad, orange parks. We'd be as conspicuous as a pair of zebras walking down Fifth Avenue arm in arm. The ship's at the airport on the opposite headland. The only way I can see to get there is to cross those parks, with their bright orange grass, in full daylight, and somehow get among those warehouses and docks along the waterfront.

"From there, we'd have to steal a car, and somehow get over to the port. Then we have to convince four lines of guardsmen that it's either bedtime, and they are sound asleep, or that we are just part of the scenery."

"It would help if their grass weren't quite such a vivid shade, or if we had orange clothes."

"God forbid; me in orange pants!"

"It's a good plan, Blake, only you need some details. Also, those swords the guards are wearing have such unpleasant waves in the edge. They look as though the genius who designed 'em had an evil disposition."

"Huh. They have compressed air guns, too."

Penton looked thoughtfully down the hallway. Two guards cluttered up the doorway, conversing interestedly. Beryllium was big news, of course. Further down the corridor, two more were equally interested in the possibility of immortality. But they were very much awake.

"You know, my friend, I wonder what these birds would do if—" Penton went through his pockets and the pouch he was still wearing. He felt his flashlight, powered by a miniature atomic disintegrator. Too miniature to do any real damage. Two packs of cigarettes that wouldn't burn in this atmosphere, which was rich in carbon dioxide and nitrogen, but too poor in oxygen to support combustion came into view. Soap, water softener, odds and ends, some pieces of magnesium scrap, and finally a small bottle of waxy, white phosphorus. "We can but try," he sighed at last.

In full view of the guards, he sat down in the middle of the room. From the flashlight, he removed the lens, the bulb, and the reflector, baring the copper contacts. From the bottle of phosphorus he removed three white sticks. Then he built up a little pile of magnesium metal on the stone flooring.

The guards had stopped talking, and were watching him uneasily. Penton had found a length of copper wire in his pocket and Blake produced another. Rapidly Penton attached them to the contacts of the flashlight, so that they extended out about three feet, a supply wand of insulated copper wire, ending in two bare bits of metal. These he wrapped around two magnesium metal nuts he found. Briefly he pressed the button of the flashlight. The magnesium nuts flared magnificently for an instant, then died as the current was broken.

The guards were drawing closer, their swords unsheathed, but looking uncertain of themselves. "Huh." Penton nodded slowly. "They are trying to make it out. Never saw an electric arc, or fire. This, I think, will be fun." He wrapped a bit of the phosphorus in a scrap of copper wire. Again the atomic flash sent a burst of flame between the contacts. This time the phosphorus came away flaring red, while an enormous cloud of dense, dirty-white smoke rolled out.

Penton and Blake slapped handkerchiefs across their noses, and ran to the water-jar on one side of the room. In a moment the room was filled with one of the most impenetrably dense, white clouds known to man.

Penton stumbled his way through the whiteness, with the protecting mask across his mouth. Outside the room, the guards were calling; inside, one was choking, coughing, and upsetting the furniture. Penton bent over his pile of magnesium metal, and a moment later a terrific flare of blue-white light glared through the enveloping pall of phosphorus pentoxide smoke. The magnesium was burning beautifully. It made a perfect camouflage.

Sixty seconds later they moved rapidly down the silent corridor; far away, around many bends, they heard the shouts of alarmed guards.

"How the blazes do you fire these pop-guns?" demanded Blake, inspecting hastily his captured weapon.

"That stud there—it isn't a nut; it's a trigger." Penton coughed and swore. "That nose mask wasn't any too effective. And my mouth is beginning to itch from the acid."

They dodged down side corridors, past doors from which bewildered Callistans appeared, to be hurled out of the path of the two Terrestrials, muscled for a far heavier world. A door appeared at the side of a corridor, and Penton halted abruptly. He caught Blake, and looked at the lettering on the door a moment.

"Damn. Wish I'd learned their writing more consciously—I think that means exit." They tried it. At their feet, a corridor slanted downward, spiraling off to the right, and down. The steep slant made running dangerous; the thin air made running difficult.

Spaced lights gave the only illumination, doors appearing occasionally gave the only indication of altitude. Down—down till one of the doors burst open, and a troop of guardsmen faced them in blank surprise. The flashlight suddenly flared with the incredible brilliance of burning magnesium, and Penton charged at the group. Blake's air gun soughed softly three times, then failed as the supply of compressed air gave out.

Stumbling over each other, the guards retreated from the weirdly flaming death Penton so evidently carried; some deadly radiation known only to these beings of another world, no doubt— The Terrestrials followed their fleeing footsteps, but turned aside at the first window. Eighty feet beneath the aperture the orange lawn swaled off toward the shabby docks and warehouses.

"Let's go," said Penton. "We can stand an eighty foot drop—I hope."

III. PIPELINE

They stood still, panting, two minutes later, lost in a maze of crated, baled goods, as the platoon of guards thundered across the broad lawn after them, running in great strides behind the Earthmen's crazy leaps. The masses of goods imported from unknown ports of this strange sea piled about them in an ordered confusion. Somewhere workmen were shouting, calling to the guards as Blake scurried around a great heap of crated fruit of some kind. Each crate was fully six feet square, and he halted abruptly.

"Penton, we need a residence. Catch hold." Blake swung at one of the bulky crates; it lifted easily to his Earth-strength. Five minutes later the guards deployed through the building, seeking, shouting, ordering. In a four-foot by six closet, completely surrounded by the friendly and uncommunicative fruit, Penton grinned thoughtfully.

"Here we are, hidden in this crate, walled in on every side by provisions, and with somewhat collapsed gastric regions, yet not taking advantage of the situation. Shall we eat?"

Blake looked at the fruit in the surrounding crates. They were about the size of lemons, with a horny-looking shell of bright purple with yellow-green spots.

"I don't know. I'm sensitive to color, and if they taste anything like they look, we'll be most remarkably ill."

"I'm not affected by color, but I am affected by food. They smell good, so I'll experiment. The soldiers seem to have missed us." Penton opened his pouch, and pawed through its contents. "Soap—I'm a cleanly individual but—say, it will grease the knife, though, when we cut this wood. Borax water softener—no help. Another scrap of magnesium—ah, here we are. The knife."

Carefully soaping the blade, he cut at the soft wood of the crate. Presently he had an opening large enough to admit his fingers, and a moment later gently extracted one of the weird-looking things. Cautiously he wiped the remaining soap from the knife blade, and attacked the horny coating. It was thin, and almost at once gave way, to allow a dark, purplish jelly to ooze forth. Skeptically Penton tested a bit of it on the point of his knife, tasted a larger amount, and smiled approval.

"Hm-m," said Blake, sampling Penton's offering. "Quite fairish. Have you any knowledge, plucked from Tha Lagth's mind as to—"

Abruptly there was a frantic scratching at the case near them, and a thunderbolt of peculiarly active flesh forced its way inward. Frantically Penton and Blake backed away in their tiny closet, beating at the furry thing half seen in the dimness. The creature, whatever it was, made a terrific leap at Penton, gripped, and sank its teeth with an unpleasant grating sound of power into the folds of the pouch he was carrying, tearing the tough fabric open instantly, to release a tinkling deluge of miscellaneous items onto the floor.

Instantly it forgot all about the men to paw frantically, with little whimpering sounds, among the wreckage. With an air of supreme triumph it came up with a small, square package, which it immediately crushed between its teeth, to consume with every evidence of the most complete satisfaction.

"My god—that was borax!" gasped Penton. "That's going to be one sick animal in a sweet short time."

Paper and package vanished as the animal gulped heavily once. Its dimly seen head turned, and gleaming, violet eyes looked up at Penton.

"Borax," it remarked pleasantly, very happily in fact. The word echoed clearly, precisely in Penton's mind, in Blake's mind, too.

Penton sat down heavily. Blake looked blankly at the animal, now sufficiently motionless for observation. It was long, two feet long. It was low, not more than six inches at the shoulder, and it had a doglike head, with rather friendly, violet eyes. But it had six short, stubby legs, each armed with four sharp claws. It was smiling, more or less, in a friendly sort of way, and displaying a set of teeth that started with glistening, grayish fangs, almost metallic in their luster, and ranged backward to a group of opposed molars as broad as a man's thumb-nail. It had a soft, gray-brown coat of fur, and a long, gently wagging tail.

"More borax?" it amended.

"I think," said Blake faintly, "that it *likes* borax, hard as that may be to believe. In fact, I think it's a mind-reading, broadcasting pooch that came because it smelled our borax."

"Like borax," mentally agreed the animal, wagging a friendly tail.

"It looks like the result of mixing a d.t.'s nightmare with a dachshund," Penton decided. "I'm glad, at least, that it doesn't like me."

"Like you," insisted the animal. "Gkrthps likes you... More borax?" The mental impressions were somewhat slurred, accented, so to speak, as the utterances of a parrot are accented by the peculiar limitations of the parrot's anatomy.

"Gk—anyway, that must be its name," Blake said. "I think we had better call it Pipeline. With all those legs, tails and heads sticking out of that unnecessarily elongated body, I think it resembles a complete network of pipes," Penton sighed. "I think—and hope—that it means it approves of me in a personal way; that is, that its liking for me and its appreciation of borax differ fundamentally. Anyway, it looks friendly."

"More borax?" telepathized the animal plaintively.

"No, Pipeline, not here. You'll have to visit us some day when we get back to the ship. There is about fifty pounds of it there."

Pipeline almost danced.

"Visit the ship... Go back to the ship."

"Hm-m, we'd like to, too, but can't just now. Say, Penton, how far do you think this creature's mental impressions reach out? Is he broadcasting our conferences here like an animated telepathic microphone? Did the Callistans send him here for that purpose?"

"Not far. I was just becoming aware of a sensation of a pleasant odor, which must have been, actually, my picking up his thoughts as he caught the scent of borax—sweet satellites, what a delicacy for any animal—when he burst in here. It doesn't radiate far. But—I have a suspicion it has a memory."

"Memory," agreed Pipeline proudly. "Remember, they must be in here... Watch the exits... No, guard the ship... You're a fool, watch the exits... You're an infernal, insubordinate, unripe idiot... You're a blistering undercaptain, trying to tell a general his duty... Get out of here before I stamp my initials permanently in your liver... Watch the ship, you blithering, blasting, blowing, brainless aberration! What did they escape for?... They want the ship... Go to the ship, visit the ship. Borax—more borax—visit the ship... They went to the ship, so why hunt the city—they'll go to the ship... Watch the ship."

Blake sighed.

"Disconnected, perhaps," he said, leaning back against a crate, "but intelligent. Highly intelligent. You are a remarkable animal, Pipeline, and you get a full pound of borax for that, the minute we reach the ship, though what you want it for, and how you live on it beats me. You seem to have a remarkable faculty for phonographic—or telepathic—recording."

He turned aside to Penton.

"I think I know how Pipeline works. His mind, I mean. Whenever we think of something, he broadcasts all he has ever heard pertaining to that subject. He's like an intelligent phonograph record—doesn't know where to stop or begin."

"Live on borax," chortled Pipeline pleasantly. "Borax necessary for this peculiar form of life... This specimen I have obtained from the watchman of a local warehouse, who reports that it was given to him, together with its mate, by a sailor returning from Stakquerl... The dissections have demonstrated the remarkable anatomy of this beast, which, unlike other life-forms, bases its fundamental life chemistry on fifty pounds of borax in the ship.

"This type of life occurs in only that one region of our planet, and is quite common there, being represented by a complete type of evolution. This is its highest representative, capable of receiving telepathic impressions direct from the mind of one man, and regenerating those thoughts in the mind of another, while only to a very limited extent understanding the material so repeated... It's a mind-reading, broadcasting pooch that came because it smelled borax... More borax?"

"Man, what a college education you got somewhere, even if you did get it a little mixed up. So you have a girlfriend, eh?"

"Girlfriend of my own." Pipeline sat down suddenly with the last two sets of legs, and stood up in front. Then lugubriously the animal lay down with the front legs, and stood up in back, while remaining seated in the middle. "No girlfriend of my own... But I have Thkrub..."

"Oh, I begin to understand. I suspect you have it the wrong way around, Ted. This is the female of the species," Blake derided.

"Female of the species bears from fifteen to fifty young at a time; the mating season is practically continuous... The male and female mate for life, and at practically any time that fifty pounds of borax in the ship is available young are produced... The lack of more borax alone prevents this extremely fecund species from overrunning the planet... They have, you observe, a series of exceedingly powerful molars, capable, in fact, of crushing minerals for digestion... The animal is capable of ingesting and utilizing inorganic boron... Let's visit the ship... They supply their energy needs, however, from the combustion of carbon compounds, as we do, being omnivorous in this respect... They make highly entertaining pets where the owner can find or procure the expensive boron compounds necessary for their life."

"Brief life history. I bet Pipeline—or is it Pipeliness—has heard that lecture a dozen times. Can you suggest a way of turning her off?"

"Turn me off, that's it... After all these years I've slaved to help you, slaved for your children, scrimped and saved so that you could have a good time, you brute... Now you turn me off for some flighty, giddy-headed—more borax?"

"No, Pipeliness, no family quarrels. You'll get borax when we get to the ship. And then only if you stay quiet until we arrive, or we ask questions. Where's your mate, Pipeliness?"

For an animal born of a small world, Pipeliness could develop speed. Penton thought this time of a male mate, and Pipeliness went to fetch him. Before either Blake or Penton could move, the animal had vanished with a soft scurry of claws.

IV. STRAGATH

"I'd never have suspected speed like that in such short legs," said Blake softly. "Do you think she'll be back?"

"More borax," sighed Penton. "Fifty pounds of borax in the ship. Man, you couldn't lose that critter now to save you. All the repressed mother-love of the last five years or so is probably welling up in her under-slung bosom. I image, from the lecture she just delivered, that friend watchman of the domestic difficulties can't feed her the boron she wants, and evidently she needs a sufficient supply of boron to have young. At any rate I need a supply of carbon compounds. She interrupted my eating rather abruptly."

"There seems to be enough jellyfruit here to keep any two people going. Tastes funny, doesn't it? Rather like a cross between orange juice and beef gravy, unpleasant as that sounds."

"It sounds omnivorous, but isn't," Penton objected. "I have a curious desire to consume some sort of meat food. They must have some kind of—what ho! They have. Or at least that certainly looks like a local substitute for the old, familiar of seashore, quick lunches."

Blake looked at the contents of the case Penton indicated. Like the one they had first raided, it was addressed to a wholesale grocer, but this contained some item that closely resembled a seven-inch hot dog.

"Even their hot dogs are skinny. Sort of in proportion," Blake pointed out. "The thing's only half as thick as it should be, and half again as long."

Penton was quietly carving at the boards of the case. Delicately he reached in, and pulled out one of the things. His brow furrowed in deep thought.

"I know what these darned things are, but for the life of me, I can't recall the name, nor the properties. I wasn't trying to learn foods when I read Tha Lagth's mind. Yes—they're food, all right. I remember that much—seems I remember eating them as is. Well here goes!"

Penton put a very small portion of the Callistan delicacy in his mouth, and bit on it gently. Blake stared. Abruptly, Penton's face froze in an expression of horrified surprise, his eyebrows climbed frantically to join his hair, then his eyes popped very wide open. He sat in frozen astonishment, while the right eyebrow slid slowly downward, and a slow, dawning comprehension spread over him. His hand, gripping the strange food, gripped tighter, and he swallowed, while his eyes closed desperately. Very slowly his Adam's apple crawled up, took hold, and slid down his windpipe with a special delivery package for his stomach.

His eyes opened, and he looked at Blake. A beatific smile spread over his face. The remainder of the thing vanished in three large gulps. Penton sat very still for a moment, as though concentrating on inner voices of surpassing beauty. Finally he looked again at Blake.

"Remarkable," he said in a falsetto voice. "Er—eh, I mean re-markable. You must try one." He pulled forth another and handed it to Blake.

Rod Blake looked at him with deep suspicion.

"Judging from the struggle you went through," he said at length, "I don't know that I'm so keen on it. Just what, my friend, was the matter with you?"

"I—I was trying to remember it. For a moment I thought I had. You see, there's a thing called *stragth* that is a kind of red sea worm, very poisonous; it stings. These are *stragath*, popularly so-called because they somewhat resemble that worm. Oh, they aren't, of course, but that's what had me scared. Try it—it's really delicious."

Blake took the thing in two fingers, very cautiously. Very cautiously, he put his teeth to a minute scrap and bit—

Instantly he dropped the thing, and jumped up. It curled violently in his grip; a thin, squealing wail of anger chattered from it through his teeth. Violently the far end of it curled up to swipe forcefully against his nose. Squealing angrily, it flopped about on the floor as Blake looked at it in undisguised horror.

Smilingly, Penton reached out and pinched the far end. It lay still—and almost simultaneously disappeared as Pipeliness darted through the crack by which she had entered before, to gobble it down in a single motion.

"More *stragath*?" she asked brightly. "More *stragath* for Thkrub?"

Behind her a somewhat larger edition scurried in, to sniff in a friendly fashion at Penton, with a wagging, silky tail. Violet eyes in a broad, mahogany-brown head looked up at him.

"Borax," said the newcomer.

Penton fished another *stragath* out of the crate, and tossed it toward the animal. "I take it you are—well, Pipeline. We won't attempt that name of yours." The bit of food was caught expertly, and vanished instantly.

"Fifty pounds of borax in the ship... Let's visit the ship," suggested Pipeline, not to be swayed from an important purpose.

"Let's change the tune, Pipeline. We have about ten kilograms of boric acid, too."

"Ten kilograms of boric acid. Let's visit the ship." Pipeliness danced happily. Abruptly her nose went up, and she trotted over to the case.

"I wondered how she made those six legs work together," Blake sighed. "Every time she's moved before, she's gone so fast they just blurred. I'm beginning to get it."

"This animal," Pipeline stated, dogmatically, following his mate, "is as are all members of this system of evolution, equipped with six pedal members... These six limbs are normally operated in the manner of a pacer, those on one side moving in unison... However, some members of the species vary this gait in almost any possible combination... Very good *stragath*."

Pipeliness sat down on her rearmost legs, on her middle legs stood up, and reached up the case with her forelegs. Long, retractile claws reached out and with an expert flip she snared a *stragath*. The thing shot through the air to be snapped up instantly by her mate. Five more followed in machine gun-like succession before she sent a stream toward her own swift-acting jaws.

"Efficient, Pipeliness, efficient. Could you send some our way?" suggested Penton. The animal glanced at him, her tail wagged briefly, and almost immediately Penton was bombarded by a rapid-fire stream of arriving *stragath*. Not quite as quick as the animals, he failed to catch all of them, and several fell to the floor. They squeaked instantly, doubled themselves the instant they hit the ground with an amazing vigor. They bounced into the air to strike hollowly against the crates above. Long before they hit the floor again, Pipeline solved the difficulty by consuming them.

Pipeliness turned violet eyes on Penton.

"Penton want *stragath*?" she asked. There was a distinct note of reproach in her communication. Penton juggled frantically with suddenly animated *stragath*, while Blake grappled with two he had caught.

"What in blazes are these? Are they food or are they animals?" The angry squawling squeak of the things was mounting rapidly as they became thoroughly aroused. Blake dropped his load to the silencing, and waiting Pipeline.

"*Stragath*," Pipeline said, "the latest triumph of modern science.... These remarkable growths are developed by the magnificent cooperation of thousands of research workers....I'll bet they ain't got a dozen and the damn things probably aren't fit to eat....Research workers combine in the ultimately perfect proportions every item of diet needed by man....Most important of all, the *stragath* soon to be marketed by Thrail Stran and Company will bring to you in delicious form these important elements in living, vital form....These advertising humbugs make me sick....I hear the damn things are alive enough so that when you jar them too much they start moving....Swell time I'll have with them chasing all around that blasted blistering warehouse....May be eaten as they naturally occur....At low temperatures they may be kept indefinitely without spoilage since they are living and hence destroy all destructive molds or bacteria....They won't smell anyway, maybe; well, you won't bring any of those things into *my* house, Grag Kuolp."

Penton sighed and sat down. He had finally succeeded in pulling Pipeliness away from the hole in the crate and had seated himself in front of it. The last of the visible *stragath* had been consumed, but still there was a persistent, faint squawling.

"Damn squealing, squawling brutes getting ready to pop...you clumsy oaf, pick up that crate," Pipeliness commented, licking a scrap of meat from her paw.

"So that's what they are," Blake said angrily. "You might have had the decency to warn me they'd kick my nose."

Penton started. "They're moving in the crate now." The squealing grew suddenly louder, much louder. It became a rapidly rising howl that, they realized, must be echoing through the whole, vast warehouse.

"They're over here." Somewhere outside a voice shouted. The heavy rhythmic tread of running guards drew nearer. Blake rose, looking at Penton.

"I think we'll have to go somewhere else."

Penton rose with his hands above his head. The crate overhead balanced on his hands, he suddenly heaved with all his power. The crate, bulky as it was, flew into the air to land with a tremendous crash somewhere beyond. Instantly, a terrific howling, squealing riot of sound started. Blake followed the crate with another, full of the quiescent *stragath*. The shock of landing broke the crate and aroused the contents.

The two Callistan dogs were incredibly active, but the *stragath* were ten thousand to one. In rapid succession, Penton crashed open four more crates.

"That may divert them," he said mildly, watching the results take form.

Penton and Blake set out hastily, entirely obscured from the sight of approaching guards by a mad, inverted snowstorm of tens of thousands of bouncing, bounding, madly cavorting *stragath*. Behind them, guards stepping on the weird things were falling in the resultant slippery mess. Blithely, the Terrestrials dodged through mountainous heaps of goods, down a long lane, finally to a small locked door. In unison, they charged it, their Earth-born strength proving too great for the frame of the exit.

* * * *

"They don't look as though they could possibly carry that load," said Penton, nodding toward the great lumbering trucks rolling down the broad traffic-choked artery that paralleled the harbor and docks. Immense trucks, almost lost under the vast heaps of merchandise loading them, rumbled by on wheels seemingly impossibly fragile. "That light gravity makes heavy loads light, and hence bulky. Bulky loads, my friend, suggest loads on which we can hide remarkably well. Won't you join me?"

A huge truckload of bagged goods of some type paused momentarily in the exigencies of traffic. A moment later it started on again. Penton and Blake pulled the huge bags of some granular, sticky substance over them.

"Must you pick sticky stuff?" grunted Blake. "Wonder how—hey, for the—hey, Ted—"

"Sh-h—" his friend clapped a restraining hand over his mouth. "I told you they wouldn't be lost easily. They just jumped on the— hey, stop it, Pipeline. My face is clean—at any rate cleaner than your tongue. What happened, couldn't you hold any more *stragath*?"

"More borax," suggested Pipeline. "More borax for Pipeliness."

For half an hour the truck rumbled on slowly, stopped and started in the slow-moving, choked traffic. Finally the truck turned, stopped a moment while something rattled noisily near them, then started again with a smooth, soundless pull of acceleration. Abruptly, the traffic noises changed, and echoing reverberations surrounded them. A Callistan called cheerily outside, and another answered him from the truck.

"It's all out," said Penton hastily. "This is the delivery point, I imagine. We'll have to put these fellows to sleep for a while, and go on—we're inside a building of some kind—phew! Must be some sort of chemical plant." Penton stirred, the sticky bag that had covered him moved, and he stood upright. Beside him, Blake rose simultaneously, and together they leaped to the ground. Four Callistans started at them in startled amazement—and slumped soundlessly to the ground after none-too-gentle taps.

They stood on the floor of an immense single room. Reaching up a hundred feet above them, and spread out three hundred feet in each direction, it was as large as three football fields, under one roof. But huge as it was, it was filled with enormous wooden tanks coated inside and out with some dark plastic material.

From the tanks, thick silvery metal pipes reached up, interconnecting in a network of conduits leading across the room. Other pipes of plastic material led to each tank from a single huge reservoir at one end of the room. Somewhere, huge blowers were whistling softly.

"Where do we go from here?" asked Blake.

"Mind your step, you blithering idiot....Grag Kuolp, some day you'll learn what I mean....Touch one of those conduits, and by the Gods of Space, electricity will tie you in knots of a hundred unpleasant varieties....Mind your step," chanted Pipeliness. "Mind your step, visit us at the fifty pounds of borax and ten kilograms of boric acid."

Penton whistled and looked into the animal's violet eyes.

"You can repeat only thoughts thunk near you, Pipeliness, but I take it you have an editorial ability—you repeat appropriate ones that make sense. You mean, I take it, that if we don't watch our steps, we won't visit the ship. Yes, you may be—Wavering Worlds, Blake— keep away from those metal things!" Penton was suddenly leaping up the wooden stairs that climbed the side of the nearest of the tanks.

Blake followed him swiftly, to pause as he neared the top. An overpowering odor of rank animal life assailed his nostrils; an odor, he realized suddenly, the great blowers had been dissipating near the lower levels. Faltering, he reached the edge of the tank and, not breathing the foul odor, looked down.

A titanic mass of warm, steaming flesh lay there, an immense, quivering vat of raw meat. Into it the silvery pipes plunged, dividing into ten thousand tendrils. Into it, the plastic tube fed a constant stream of frothy, bubbling liquid. From that another plastic tube drew a constant stream of putrid-smelling fluid. Nauseated, Blake stumbled away, down the wooden steps. A moment later, Penton, his face greenish in hue, followed him. But the latter immediately started off across the great room to a small space on one side, where men had evidently been intended to work.

Blake found him staring at a clear, glassy panel, some ten by ten feet, connected with the silvery tubes and the maze of plastic tubes, fitted with dials, valves, gauges, and wheel-controls.

"By the Nine Gods of the Nine Worlds, and the multiple deities of space!" Penton breathed. "These men—Blake, my lad, do you know what that is?" Penton bent forward, looked at bars, pipes, instruments and sighed. He turned around, gaping in awe. "That, my boy, is a power house. It generates power at about 1000 volts D.C."

"Which can, of course, be raised by the addition of further cells in series," interrupted the beast at their side. "The greatest difficulty is the size required to obtain practical amperages....This can be done, however....Take that animal out, if you will, Purthal....That's the third time it's wandered in here....It belongs in Farg Thorun's lecture room....This can be done, as I was saying, now blast you, stay where you belong before I throttle you," Pipeline concluded.

Blake stared. "Electric eels—they have 'em trained!"

"No, those aren't animals—they're synthetic life made to serve the function. This is where they get the power for the electric mechanism of half the city. I imagine, for such services as electric controls, telephones, radio, telegraph.

"But look, Blake. The operator of this plant must be a well paid technician, and should, I imagine, have a private car. It must be in the building somewhere. I'll look down near the door the truck came in; you see if it's toward the back." Penton started toward the doorway as Blake trotted toward the dim-lit rear of the huge room. Pipeline and his mate looked at them uncertainly, then split, each following one of the two men.

Penton found the vehicle, a small, smooth-lined sedan-type car, parked between two of the giant, wooden tanks.

"Blake—" he called out. Faintly, from the far end of the room he heard his friend's answer.

"Rod, look over that switchboard, and figure out which are the mains leading the power out to the city, and open those switches. I wouldn't cut off the blowers, or the circulating pumps. That electric-flesh stuff might get peeved and climb out. I'll look over the car."

V. MUSCLEMOBILE

Five minutes later Blake found him sitting on the door ledge of the car with Pipeline before him. He looked up at Blake and shook his head. "These Callistans are the super-past-masters of the grand craft of life-molding. Take a look at the engine." Blake glanced at the car, and noted that it was evidently rear-engined. A moment later he had the hood up and was looking at the mass of mechanism.

"Looks like a six-cylinder radial type, equipped with a supercharger—but it's made out of plastics. Something like the one we rode in—and wrecked—on Ganymede."

"Huh," grunted Penton. "Almost the whole car is. It's got a metal frame, but on a fireless world metal is costly. Plastics, weight for weight, are nearly as strong. This isn't painted blue; it is blue."

"The engine isn't. It looks like green glass."

"I think I pointed out that even a Diesel couldn't work in this air? That, my boy, is not an engine. That is an animal, a nice, synthetic animal."

"*Animal!* A six-cylinder animal? With a gear-box and ignition system?"

"No, six-muscled animal. The supercharger is not a supercharger; it's a blower, a mechanical lung. The fuel tank contains not gasoline, but a sugar solution. I tasted it. The ignition system, on the other hand, is made up of synthetic nervous tissue, and a few, miniature electric cells for stimulation. Muscles, my friend, don't need a high oxygen concentration; they repair themselves, renew themselves, and grow stronger with use.

"I didn't have time to look, but I suspect that the animal engine also has a series of synthetic kidneys to remove waste products, and probably some oil-secreting cells, like the oil glands in your elbow, to supply lubrication. Six muscles pulling on tendons connected to a slip-ring—probably made of non-poisoning silver—a metal crankshaft geared direct to the wheels. The speedometer reads to the equivalent of eighty miles an hour; about the speed of a greyhound in good training."

Blake looked thoughtfully at the streamlined vehicle.

"I wonder, would it answer to the name of Rover, do you suppose?"

"No, but it would answer to the controls, which consist of nerve tissue stimulated by small levers. The steering mechanism consists of four muscles working the front wheels." Penton sighed. "Rod, we Terrestrials never began to guess what life could be made to do. A muscle is three times as efficient as a gas engine, and so far as weight per horsepower goes—your thigh muscle weighs ten pounds, works at the wrong end of a 10 to 1 lever, and can still lift three hundred pounds. I've seen you do it. That's a pull of 3000 pounds from a ten-pound lump of watery, almost substanceless jelly."

"But, oh, my friend, how tired that muscle can get. And it doesn't move me any eighty miles an hour—even when P'holkuun and his whole tribe were after me, and I was entreating it to do so," Blake pointed out.

"What you need is a mechanical lung with plenty of capacity, like that blower, and a plastic heart, like that centrifugal pump I noticed. The muscles of your heart work indefinitely without stopping because their blood supply is adequate. Even a gasoline engine gets tired if you stick a potato in the exhaust pipe and clog it up with waste products.

"But the important point is this: If you feel convinced you can walk faster than this thing can go, walk—I'm riding. You can, however, do the driving, if you like. Your legs are longer, and I must admit that this was designed for an eight-footer. I'll show you the system." Penton paused a moment. Sounds were floating through the still-open door through which the truck had brought them. "Hm-m-m—I think you must have upset the traffic light system from the sound."

"There did seem to be an argument among the truck drivers as I came over here. I wondered about that. Of course, we don't mind an accident or two, but even this muscle-bound leaping Lena won't crawl over those trucks. Just how did you plan to help us make speed across the city by plugging traffic hopelessly?"

"Get in, and we'll start. I'll show you what I had in mind." Penton grinned. Pipeline and Pipeliness tumbled over Penton as he climbed in after Blake. Cautiously Blake tested the controls, a little lever running back and forth in a slot, a transverse bar that controlled direction, a single foot pedal that applied a friction brake. The car moved forward with a steady, smooth thrust as he advanced the lever in the slot.

The wheels turned, and they were driving out through the great door. Trucks, blocks of huge trucks stood in the street, bleating feebly on high-pitched horns that echoed unhappily in the thin air. The soft whine of the blower under them was scarcely audible.

"You can get through with this small car where those bulky things can't—er, wiggle a muscle. Turn right when you get out of this drive, and make time."

Five small cars loaded with uniformed guards were weaving through the lines of stalled trucks, sirens howling angrily. A path was opening up slowly, with much backing, twisting and turning on the part of the trucks.

"I think I'll park," suggested Blake, pulling to the curb.

The guards rushed by them, heading, very evidently, for the power house. More guards were rushing up from the opposite direction. Several more carloads, in fact.

"Nice of them." Blake grinned, putting the car in motion again with a smooth, soundless rush. "They've opened a path for us."

"I hoped they would." Penton nodded. "Keep—"

"Hey—Ted—" Blake slowed the car savagely, cursing bitterly. "You back-handed idiot, we're headed the wrong way. That's the Assembly Building we just got out of up there."

"I was worried for a minute. Get going. Naturally it is; how did you hope to get through four successive lines of guardsmen? Four, very alert, very thoroughly organized lines? This place here, I hope, and suspect, is not guarded. Did you happen to recall that this is the one place on the planet where they *know* they won't find us? And that the failure of the power plant called all the guards available at headquarters for soothing innumerable traffic snarls, and other duties.

"And do you suppose they stopped to remember that we had two ultra-violet guns and two dis-guns in those spacesuits? Not so, my lad. And forty lines of alert guardsmen won't argue with four weapons like that.

"You may drop me at the window there. Sure—the fence is ornamental and made of wood—I know. I haven't yet had a chance to get out all the splinters that remind me that I didn't quite jump over it."

Blake, smiling broadly, swung the car. The light wooden fence surrounding the broad, parked lawn dissolved in a hail of flying splinters as the car shot up the rise to the white stone building, its wheels skidding on slippery, crushed grass. It paused a moment under the huge windows, twenty feet from the ground, while Penton stepped out.

Four guardsmen stepped out of a door two hundred feet away, to see Penton flying upward in a leap that brought him to the window ledge. The guards retreated before the angry charge of a half ton of automobile. Their compressed air guns sent slugs that rebounded uselessly from the tough, thick plastic of its windows.

"The most recent weapon of civil defense," stated Pipeline dogmatically, "is expected to end the reign of automobile bandits. This vehicle, made entirely of hard metals instead of plastics, is mounted on six wheels, each individually powered by its own motor of nine muscles....Capable of a speed of nearly one hundred and fifty kilometers an hour it won't do any good....Those bandits haven't got any respect for life at all and they'll probably hold up your warehouse one of these days....Get up....I have to—"

Blake noted the cause of these remarks. It was made of metal, gray, hard metal. It had six smaller thick windows, and six large heavy wheels, under humped, bulging motors. Muscles or not, they drove the thing at a crazy pace, straight for the little car. Blake dodged desperately. The charging behemoth swerved angrily, its heavy, protruding ram held toward him steadily.

Six nine-muscled motors gave it acceleration almost equal to that of the light vehicle; a Callistan driver in a Callistan vehicle gave it the needed edge. Desperately Blake streaked along the wall of the building, almost in front of the heavy, armored car. Avoiding the dangerous, direct attack that Blake had hoped would pile it against the stout, stone wall, it paralleled his track, to squeeze him against the wall. Desperately he braked, hoping it would overshoot.

The light car swerved, wagged almost, on slippery grass, front wheels locked far to the right. The heavier car tore through the slippery surface to gravel beneath; it held parallel to him exactly. Brakes off, and with the control at full speed ahead, the blower whined in sudden speed. The wheels slipped, gripped, and Blake's car leaped forward. Six-wheel drive gave the heavier car the edge, and only Earth-trained quickness of perception enabled Blake to reverse, slew completely around, and start madly back from the trap before the other was after him. Desperately he tore off across the lawn, glancing at the rear-vision mirror. Speed—perhaps in speed—

There was an enormous black mushroom sprouting there on the lawn. Blake slowed gently and turned around. An enormous mushroom of impalpable dust, settling very slowly in even this thin air. And a huge cavity, twenty feet across and unguessably deep where the armored car had been. Slowly Blake drove back toward the neat, round hole that had appeared in the wall of the Assembly Building. Penton climbed into the car.

"They have the telephones working again," he said cheerfully. "I don't think you did a very good job on the power plant. Here are your guns." Penton adjusted his somewhat, and put the blunt, heavily insulated muzzle against the windshield. A neat, round hole appeared, large enough to allow the gun's passage. Presently a duplicate port graced the side window. "But it's not all to the bad. As it is the airport officials will know what the disintegrator did to that armored car. I don't think they'll argue."

"The telephones working, eh?"

"Yes, somebody in a pink jacket with pale blue pants was yelling into one that all the guards were blind. I gave 'em a light dose of UV. They'll be all right in an hour. He was getting an answer, too."

* * * *

Blake looked down. Callistans were slowly filtering back to the airport they had so recently and hastily deserted. The vast traffic snarl of the city was slowly straightening out as the power plant went back into operation, and signal lights, telephones and radios went back to work.

"They've formed what guards can still see around that metal you left," he reported. "I hope they are grateful."

"I know. We didn't have to leave it, but on the other hand, why not? We had those spare plates, about five hundred pounds of beryllium. They can get started, and treat older people, the sick, with the life-cells they can create with that. And—somehow, Rod, I want to keep friendly with those people. When we do get back to Earth, the things they can teach us will be worth knowing, and they are, fundamentally, a pretty decent bunch."

"Pretty decent bunch," agreed Pipeline, very proudly. Only Blake could turn around; Penton was busy at the controls. He was silent for some seconds, then he spoke softly.

"Ted, my friend, we better make time for Ganymede."

"Ganymede? P'holkuun—" Penton started.

"And the *shleath*. No, we weren't popular. But we will be, we will be. Did you happen to think that no *shleath* could possibly digest Pipeline? Pipeline is made of boron. But Pipeline, on the other hand, would probably enjoy a meal of—"

"More borax?" hopefully suggested Pipeline.

"God forbid!" said Blake hastily. "*Shleath*, lots more *shleath*."

Penton looked up at Blake suddenly, and grinned.

"You are right, by Jupiter, they can! A *shleath* can't digest boron, of course, and they can destroy the *shleath*—but they can't! There are thousands of *shleath*, more—"

"Borax," pleaded Pipeliness. Somehow it sounded weak, and very satisfied.

"*You*," said Blake very softly, "don't know. The prof on Callisto said they were a very fecund race. If I had known, had I guessed what he meant, they would have got no borax on *this* ship. As it is—all I can suggest is that we hurry. Two Pipelines in this ship are pleasant, but—"

Slowly Penton looked down. Pipeliness was sitting proudly, if somewhat crampedly among some fifty, three-inch-long, six-legged, furry animals.

Fifty minute, friendly tails waved in pleasure.

"Borax?" suggested fifty small, very friendly, mental voices.

"No," said Penton softly, but very definitely. "Not, my friends, by a damn sight. Not until we hit Ganymede."

THE TENTH WORLD

I. SHLEATH vs. PIPELINE

Cautiously, Penton looked around the corner of the building. In the west, Jupiter was setting; here, on Ganymede, complete darkness would come in a few moments.

"No one in sight," he whispered. "For God's sake, don't start concentrating, Blake. Those boys are catching on to telepathy too fast. If they don't hear us, they may telepath us if you think so blasted hard. Hurry up."

Blake hitched his pack into a more comfortable position, and the two set off hurriedly, noiselessly down the broad, deserted avenue. Two blocks they passed silently, to turn down a narrow, rubbish-choked alley. Jupiter's light faded altogether, and they had to pick their way with utmost care. Six blocks they traversed without disturbance—then abruptly a squeaking flurry of shuffling, running steps darted out from under some rubbish. Dim light reflected from the clouded sky overhead showed a two-foot, glistening mass of evilly furious protoplasm racing down the alley toward them, squealing in helpless fury.

Behind it, silent as death, but with a broad grin of eagerness on its homely face, came a six-legged creature built on the general lines of a dachshund. The protoplasm darted under some rubbish; the six-legged dog clawed after it, the piled boards exploding in a dozen directions, to fall with a furious clatter.

There was a moment of savage squalling, and sodden gulping sounds, while the two men shrank back into protecting shadows. Somewhere a window went up, and a Lanoor's voice shrilled curses into the silence of the night.

* * * *

The six-legged animal came out from the mass of rubbish presently, its head high, walking with a slow, rather labored step. Its belly had expanded miraculously, until the six short legs barely held it from the ground. Its keen nose detected the man, and, for a moment, it sniffed at them briefly, tail wagging, before it went on about its business. Two more of the animals trotted down the alley alertly, paused a moment to watch the first, and turned away disappointed.

"One of Pipeline's innumerable progeny can make more noise chasing down a *shleath*, than any single animal I ever before encountered," Blake said with intent bitterness. "Can we move now, do you think?"

"It isn't the hexapods, it's the *shleath* that do the squalling." Penton reproved him.

"It wasn't the *shleath's* idea to throw that lumber around. From what I saw, its primary interest was getting under there and staying, very quiet and peaceable."

"Shut up and move. Somebody may come to see if the *shleath* were all eaten, or only part. We have to get out of here while we can—" Penton turned down the next intersecting street; together they dodged through the sleeping city. Half a mile they went, then gradually, as they neared the airport, more life appeared. Ships from cities half around the world, and still in daylight, were active, and the air force crew had to be up.

"Man, what I'd give for some of those sleep-gas bombs they used on us the first time we landed," sighed Penton. "There's a dozen Civil Guards standing about our spaceship."

"You said you'd get through somehow." Blake shrugged. "Get going. It's almost light."

Penton glowered at him, and sat down in the shadow of a low, spreading, bushlike tree. From the knapsack he carried, he pulled a number of small metal chips and cuttings, piled them on the sidewalk before him, and added a handful of filings. Then two waxy white cylinders half an inch through and three inches long. He rose to his feet and nodded toward Blake.

"All right, guy, get moving."

A flash of electric current snapped from an atomic flashlight in his hand, touched the metal chips, and they burst into sudden, intense flame. Penton ran hastily into deeper shadows in the direction of the airport. The flare built up to a colossal, intolerable glare; voices over at the airport shouted, and gangling, seven-and-a-half-foot Lanoor Civil Guardsmen were racing toward the strange beacon.

Penton and Blake raced in the opposite direction. Every eye was focused on the weirdly brilliant flare Penton had just made. Windows were clattering open in nearby houses, curious voices calling out. The Earthmen slipped down the side of the huge hangar, rounded a turn, and jumped to their ship. In an instant, Penton had the lockdoor open, and was struggling at the inner door.

The combination dial delayed him, slow turns that must be accurate.

"The flare's burned out," Blake said softly. "They—" A sudden new shout went up, and the Civil Guards were streaming back across the field toward them, their arms waving frantically. From the nearer barracks, a score of Guardsmen burst out, half-dressed and holding up dragging clothes with one hand, blunt weapons waving in the other.

A monstrous eye winked lazily, redly, across the field at them, then opened fully in a blinding pencil of light that pinned them like insect specimens on the broad, blue-green turf of the flying field.

The inner door opened as Penton threw a lever. Simultaneously the outer door swung shut on rubber grommets. A score of men shouting outside were suddenly silenced. Penton dived through the widening crack, twisted up the main corridor to the control room.

A moment later the atomic engines *tchked* twice in gentle reproof as relays closed, and began to sing softly of empty spaces. The ship trembled slightly, and when Blake reached the window, a patchwork field was dwindling swiftly below. A dozen, then a score of great beams of light laced across the city, swinging back and forth in slow majesty.

* * * *

Penton settled back in the pilot seat comfortably, with a deep sigh. He snapped on the automatic controls, and hauled the knapsack off his back.

"Was I mistaken, or did I see Pipeline making a mad dash to join us just before we left?"

Blake chuckled.

"You weren't mistaken, but I guess the borax did the trick. The greedy little hog couldn't leave to follow us until he had eaten it all. But I told you he'd find where we were going."

Penton smiled. "Maybe," he punned, "a hexapod can trail a man by his sense, the way a bloodhound trails a man by his scents. They have telepathic power."

Blake looked at him sourly.

"Lousy, if I may say so. Are any planes trying to follow us?"

Penton shook his head.

"Not now. We're about fifty miles up, and going farther rapidly—ah, there's the sun." A burst of light struck through the control window as the spaceship shot out of the shadow of Ganymede. "Poor P'holkuun. In some ways it seems like a sort of dirty trick. The poor guy's been sweating for three days over that speech thanking us for exterminating the *shleath*."

Blake groaned.

" 'Farewell—come again—we've been glad to see you.' That's all right. But when an orator works himself into a foaming frenzy and calls us the 'saviours of our civilization' and 'the destroyers of the tyrannous Shaloor overlords,' to wind up in a burst of rhetorical glory on 'the greatest, the final blessing, the gift of the hexapods which have freed us from the terrible menace of the *shleath*'—I quit. Personally, I'll bet P'holkuun was glad to be quit, too. I like that guy, blue-haired beanpole or not, and I'll bet he was no happier trying to prepare that speech than we were trying to work up nerve enough to sit through it. I—hey—we're on the daylight side of Ganymede."

Penton rose a bit in his seat, and looked down through the window, thoughtfully.

"So we are. Also, if you observe carefully, getting further toward that side. I'm going to step up to a full Earth-normal acceleration, so grab hold."

The ship was suddenly pulling harder, as the acceleration increased from only slightly more than the equal of Ganymedian gravity to equal Earth's gravitational acceleration.

"My Lord, I'm heavy," Blake grunted. His feet seemed strangely stuck to the floor, and as he walked across the room, his motions were curiously jerky. "Three months on that light world plays hell with your sense of timing.

"But look—we're on the *daylight* side of Ganymede. And Jupiter off there, and there's Callisto and the rest—well, for where are we bound?"

Penton looked at him for a moment, frowning, then a light seemed to dawn. His expression showed only annoyed disgust.

"For the love of space. Now I get it. The Tenth World, of course."

"Which," Blake pointed out, "is outside of Pluto's orbit—further from the Sun. Since we started from the night side of Ganymede, and are now on the day side, we're heading *toward* the sun, not away from it. Or, to bring up an old stickler, was Loshthu a *thushol*, not a real Martian—"

"In either case he'd be a real Martian, since a *thushol* is just as truly a Martian animal as is the centaur," Penton pointed out, "but you are just slightly off the track. We are headed toward the sun. Jupiter and the Tenth World are on opposite sides of the sun at the particular moment, if those Martian records weren't wrong, and I haven't made too many slips covering the transformations."

"Oh," said Blake softly. "Did you find out just where and what it was? You didn't tell me much."

"You were too busy playing with the food for the ship. The Martian expedition to Pluto first spotted it—the two planets happened to be nearly in conjunction then, and they have a good orbit calculation. It's in terms of Martian days, hours, minutes, and years, though. I don't know what day, hour and minute it is on Mars. I made rough calculations, and know about where the planet is, which is what we will have to go on. It was never visited, but it's five and two-thirds billions of miles out."

Blake whistled.

"I'm gonna get out my asbestos pants—and not because I am afraid of heat. What will the temperature be?"

"The Martians figured it to be about ten to twelve degrees above zero."

"*Above zero?*" Blake exclaimed. "What is it, radioactive heat, or what?"

"No, solar heat. The zero, however, is zero absolute. Minus which there is no minus, which is why that planet's not minus."

"I like swimming, so maybe an asbestos bathing suit for swimming in liquid hydrogen is called for." Blake grinned.

"You'll need something more than asbestos; you'll need an anti-gravity swimming suit. Liquid hydrogen is so light a liquid that nothing either solid or liquid will float in it, and even some gases would sink."

"Say, I just thought—if it's the far side of the sun we are headed for, how long is it going to take? Half a billion miles from Jupiter's satellites to the sun, and then ten times farther out to Ten."

"Not long. Sixty days or so. We'll be busy, I think, making over the spacesuits for atomic heating and so forth, checking over the ship, which hasn't had an overhaul since we started out, and so on. Also—"

"At Earth-gravity acceleration, make it in sixty days? When will we stop moving, though?"

"That includes stopping. Thirty days or so accelerating, thirty slowing. If you use Earth-acceleration for thirty days, my lad, you build up a most unholy velocity. If it weren't that we'll be well out in the edges of the Solar System when we hit our top, I wouldn't dare.

"But you go on and take an off-shift now. I'll wake you in eight hours, and you can take over. I want to check my lines and accelerations, anyway."

Blake rose with a sigh.

"O.K., Ted. Nothing I can do for you now? Want some coffee— sandwiches—something like that?"

"Thanks, no. Go ahead, sleep."

II. THE TENTH PLANET

Blake looked at the gadget doubtfully.

"Proton projector—so that's what you were trying to do? But what in blazes do you want it for now that you've made it? It kicks like a steer."

Penton nodded, ruefully rubbing a sore wrist.

"It isn't quite that bad. I just forgot—it's easy to think a ray-gun won't kick."

"It's a wonder to me that you didn't electrocute yourself. I still don't see why you don't wind up with an electron charge that'd be enough to make a lighting bolt say 'please.' "

Blake raised the clumsy-looking weapon, pointed it toward the heavy steel target place and pressed the discharge button skeptically. The air cleft opened before the mad flight of the protons driven forth, glowing in a path reaching toward the heavy steel target plate and pressed the discharge weapon kicked back under the drive that shot forth the massive protons at close to 100,000 miles a second.

Abruptly, the steel plate glowed with a hazy, violet light. Ripping static discharges smashed down from it, and the metal hissed like water suddenly touched by a red-hot iron. The steel vaporized into gas, glowing with an intolerable light that faded away gradually.

Blake lowered the weapon.

"Not too bad. Knowing the kick was coming, it didn't bother much more than an extra-heavy .45, but I still don't see the advantage. Half a mile range in air, while the UV pistol doesn't kick, fires continuously, and has a five mile range. The dis gun has a seven mile range, doesn't kick, and allows no argument—anything that tries to argue simply ceases to exist. Why this?"

Penton grinned.

"In about two hours we are going to land on Planet Ten. First men to do so, and we ought to learn a little about its rocks, etc. What strange minerals form at -265° C.? What elements are available?

"Do you remember, my lad, the famous analytical work you pulled on Venus? We'd used up most of our salt, because I forgot to pack that fifty pound bag before we started. And so we were going to collect some on Venus.

"And you announced that the salt of the sea water contained no poisonous elements, but was nearly all sodium chloride. Bright lad. We used some, innocently, and by good luck used it while in the ship. How many hours was it we spent in dreamland? And oh, man, were you utterly soused when you did wake up! Staggered like a rundown gyroscope, talked like a guy who'd lost his false teeth. Sodium chloride, you said. No poisonous elements. And treated us to a quintuple dose of sodium bromide!"

"Well, damn it, bromide and chloride act so darned much alike, I wasn't the first man to get fooled. I said it was only qualitative—answered all those tests—"

"Sure it did. Except it put us in dreamland for thirty-six hours straight. And we wound up with bromide intoxication, it took us four days more to get over. It was lucky we had some salt left.

"I'm not blaming you," Penton disclaimed. "I'm just explaining. It wasn't until we tried the spectroscope that we caught on to just what was the matter. As chemists and geologists, we're hams, but, by the gods, we can read a spectrum. You can't analyze with a UV gun because it messes all the lines hopelessly. You can't analyze with a disintegrator, because it doesn't leave anything to analyze. Hence, this gadget; the iron vapor it raised just then was swell material for a spectroscope.

"But look; this planet's about 15,000 miles in diameter, I believe. We're headed now for the equatorial, the hot zone. It must be all of 5°

above absolute zero there. Helium may be a gas, but everything else in the Universe is a solid at that temperature. Suppose you start your breakfast, and my lunch, and I'll finish checking the decelerations. We seem to be heading for an immense plain, which may make landing easier. Did you notice this planet had a moon? It's 1,000,000 miles out, and 2,000 miles in diameter."

Blake turned for the galley as Penton put a few last touches on the proton gun, and put away the tools. Three times, while Blake was trying to get the meal, Penton sounded the acceleration change warning, and Blake had to cram things hastily into the non-spilling acceleration containers. Once however, he chased a fried egg about the galley with a frying pan for half a minute before a violent acceleration brought it to roost. In bitter silence, he removed it from his chest, and opened another into the pan.

Beyond the lockdoor lay the utterly bleak surface of the Tenth World. A dim, frozen plain stretched out to a far horizon lost in the pressing darkness of this far, raveling edge of the Solar System. Low in the east, the rising sun was a brighter star, an intolerably brilliant, dimensionless point of light, casting a light that seemed little brighter than moonlight on Earth. But it was bleak, utterly cheerless light. And it was cold, cold.

Barely visible to one side was a lake of clear, sparkling, slightly bluish liquid. Tiny, starlit waves danced and glittered on its surface, moved by some thin, cold wind of this frozen outcast world.

A chill finger from Death's homeland reached into the lock, and Blake shivered violently. He advanced the heat control at his belt.

"Great God, it's cold!" he exclaimed, teeth chattering.

Penton's laughter ticked metallically in his radio receiver.

"Step out, brother Blake, step out into the breeze. Into the warm sunlight and the bright and warm starlight."

Blake rounded the hull of the ship, resting on a smooth patch of sparse, blue sand over black, angular pebbles. There was an end to the plain here. The lake nestled almost at the foot of an immense, chalky cliff that towered into starlit dimness overhead. Off to the north, and vanished, heading, as they knew, to a greater river, part of a yet greater one that emptied finally into a huge, inland sea.

Around the curve of the ship, from the peak of the chalky cliff, a stream of liquid was arching downward, spraying, breaking into flying droplets in the thin air of the frozen world, an air consisting only of helium, and the vapors of this liquid—hydrogen. Nearly a thousand feet it hurled itself down, to smash in glittering foam on broken debris fallen from the huge cliff.

Off to the right, a vein of dark rock shot up at an angle through the cliff, and broke off sharply. A thinner vein of a gray stone lay beneath it. Near the base of the cliff in that direction, the tumbled debris lay on the bluish, sandy beach, jumbled, rounded rock, jet black in the light of a five-and-three-quarters-billion-mile distant sun.

The great cliff stretched off, off to the right for unending distances, lost in the dimness that shrouded forever the far reaches of this dead world.

"Magnificent," sighed Penton, "but not beautiful. Let's go over toward that dark part of the cliff."

Two miles they followed the little lake's shore, then a quarter of a mile down the meandering stream that led from it. The little stream split, and split again in passing a group of tiny islands of the gritty, blue sand, subdivided in a series of streams less than three feet wide. Cautiously Penton tested the solidity of the sandy stuff under his booted foot. Then he stepped across, stepped again, and once more.

"Come ahead, Blake. It's easy enough."

"Catch," called Blake, and heaved the camera across to Penton. He followed Penton's cautious steps. "Hey, what in blazes is this sand? It doesn't feel right." Safely on the other side, he bent to pick up a handful in his thick gloves. Slowly, as he watched, it vanished.

"That," said Penton, "is solid oxygen, I believe. Just what that chalky cliff is, I am not sure, but nitrogen is my guess. Glaciers of it. The sand out across the way is also, I suspect, solid oxygen. The darker rock under it is just plain, ordinary rock."

The black rock glinted under the faint silver light of an immensely distant, heatless sun.

"That light is just strong enough to show how bleak this place is. There isn't even snow to cover its bare bones."

Penton nodded.

"It rains quite frequently, I imagine. Rains liquid hydrogen. In the course of ages, that rain has washed all the snow into the rivers and oceans, and now it's piled up in mountain ranges. Like that." His head nodded grotesquely in his transparent helmet, bowing toward the chalky cliff of frozen nitrogen. "I'm going to test that black rock."

Penton set up the camera with Blake's help, then leveled the proton gun and fired at the huge vein of black rock that jutted up. The rock flamed into an inferno of heat, swirled madly in tornadoes of protons, and relapsed into scintillating vapor. Penton pressed the trigger of the camera with a clumsy, gloved finger.

"Now, the greenish-gray—"

"Penton," said Blake faintly, "did you notice those rounded rocks?"

Ted Penton turned his eyes toward his friend.

"Yes, there are hundreds of 'em—all over. I'm going to test—"

"They moved," stated Blake. "I saw 'em."

Penton looked at him thoughtfully.

"You saw shadows. That swirling gas—"

"They," said Blake pointedly, "*are* moving."

Penton looked closely toward one of the ten-foot, irregularly rounded boulders. Very, very slowly it was changing its shape. A dozen near it were changing shape. As they changed, they rolled slowly, irregularly toward the dying glow in the rocky cliff-face.

"Great guns!" gasped Penton. "They—they're *alive!*"

Blake yelled and jumped clumsily under the heavier gravity. Penton turned with leveled proton gun, then lowered it slowly. Blake was heading rapidly toward a narrow, deep crevice in the wall of the cliff, a fault between two immense masses of the solid, black rock. Behind him, rolling very slowly over the spot where he had stood, a ten-foot "boulder" stopped indecisively, changed shape slowly, flattening into stability.

"If you must yell, Rod," said Penton sharply, "disconnect your transceiver first. They can't move fast enough to catch anything, so come out of hiding."

Blake came out of the deep crevice sheepishly. "It startled me, damn it. Hell, it's enough of a shock to see a boulder start walking, but when the darned thing suddenly touches you from behind—"

He stopped, then turned and raced madly for the little series of islands giving access to the far side of the stream and lake, where the ship rested. Penton stared, then followed the direction of Blake's eyes.

From out of the dimness beyond the horizon of the vast plain, *something* was coming. Dozens of Things. No creeping slowness, but a savage, swift motion. Immense Things in incredible action on an impossible world. From dimness that stretched to unseen horizons, they rolled up. Already Blake had fled halfway to the tiny islands that served as stepping stones.

"Blake, stop, you won't make it," he warned. "Come back." Blake's labored running slowed to a halt. Then his instinctive, quick-calculating mind summed up the situation. With equal speed he re-joined Penton.

"From the looks of things, let's head for the crevice there." He panted. "And pray God they go for us instead of the ship."

"We're all right, I think. We can wait on this side of the lake. What in God's name are they—I never saw a vehicle like that before."

The vast Things were slowing down somewhat and came into clearer focus now. Sunlight showed them only vaguely, huge things, a hundred feet long and thirty in diameter, immense cylinders of utter, jet black rolling swiftly across the level plain. Their very blackness made them almost invisible against the dark plain. They were black with the blackness of space itself; an utter, total absorption of every ray of light that struck them.

The first rolled up, hitching itself strangely to curve its path.

"The ship," said Penton tensely. "They're after the ship. I won-der—" He leveled the proton projector, and pressed the button. A slim, solid line of glowing light lanced out across the tiny lake, and struck the vast thing of blackness. Instantly it recoiled. A spot of furious in-candescence boiled on its side, a spot twenty feet across. It quivered into motionlessness.

A strange limpness came over it, and simultaneously the jet black-ness left it, replaced by a slate-blue color. It deflated like a balloon just needled, flattening out until one edge touched the lake of hydrogen. The liquid boiled furiously, hissing violently. Clouds of vapor rolled up, to be whipped away by the thin, keen wind.

The second and third and fourth changed their courses and rolled swiftly, not toward the ship, but toward the slate-blue hulk that slumped like a dropped cylinder of putty on the shore. Black bulks squirmed over it, hiding it.

Half a dozen others had arrived. They squirmed vainly for a place beside the dead thing, and rolled on away toward the ship. Penton's pro-ton gun lanced out again, again—five times. Five huge things writhed, then slumped in death, steaming faintly. Others piled on them. Franti-cally, Blake joined in the slaughter. Scores, hundreds of the beasts rolled up from dimness, sailing madly, blithely into death and destruction. Wildly they piled against the dead bulks of their brothers, hiding the slaty carcasses under heaving, whale-like masses of jet flesh.

Penton sighed at last and lowered his gun.

"Stop, Blake," he said. "It's useless. There are hundreds more coming and our guns are about exhausted. I get it now. They'll just come from all over that plain. It's heat."

"Heat?"

"They're living animals and they live on it." Penton nodded wearily. "Just pray that the ship's up to it. We built her with a powerful frame, and there's only a certain number of those brutes can touch her at once."

"But—why? They're utterly unafraid—"

"They have nothing to be afraid of—or never have had. They don't understand fear. Look. Ten of them on the ship now. Will it take it—"

The huge bulks squirmed and writhed their way over each other, over the ship. Others pushed and squirmed in faintly audible squealings and gruntings, seeking to reach the warm metal sides of the ship.

"Heat," Penton sighed. "They must live on it. They're warm-blooded—boiling-blooded, you might almost say. Somehow, that black hide of theirs is heat-proof while they're alive but releases its heat when they die. Look, they're leaving that first one we killed. It's frozen solid."

III. MIND OVER MATTER

Blake looked thoughtfully toward the huge, shapeless mound that surmounted their little spaceship.

"You know, we made that ship strong as blazes. It'll stand an awful strain, but I don't know that it will stand that strain when the metal's been made brittle by this temperature. And—if that ship is broken down— Well, the Martians were the last people even to see this planet, let alone visit it!"

"It won't break," Penton said decisively. "The atomic engines are fueled for about twelve months, and until their power gives out, the currents we established in the walls will prevent it from cooling. That's not what's bothering me, though. What I want to know is how we are going to get in. Just go over and nudge one of those little land whales and say, 'Would you step aside for a moment, sir, while we move in?' "

"We're hot," said Blake, "and I don't mean we're good. If we get anywhere near them, they'll probably start trying to cuddle with us. They—"

"Will," said Penton, looking behind him. "They've spotted us."

A half-dozen of the bulks stirred uneasily, switching, and moving clumsily. Then, broadside on, they started rolling toward the two men on the most direct line—through the lake of liquid hydrogen.

"They'll drown in that," pronounced Blake.

"Or freeze. I—" Penton stopped. The first one had rolled into the liquid, sending it splashing in rainbow showers of ultra-cold. It rolled smoothly on into the lake, going deeper and deeper, until it was fully twenty feet deep in the stuff. Then, it stopped. Blake stared open-mouthed as the huge, blunt end of the vast cylinder of apparently brainless flesh split. As though hinged, an immense, thick flap of black, leathery hide rolled down, and instead of the leathery, featureless cylinder-end, a whole assortment of organs appeared.

First was a tube, fully two feet in diameter, that shot out like an elephant's trunk, to dip into that inconceivably frigid lake. The mobile liquid swirled and bubbled, twisting in vortices. With a tremendous smack, audible in even that thin, chill air, the tube broke contact with the surface of the liquid.

"Drinking," gargled Penton, "drinking liquid hydrogen. By the Nine—Ten Tumbling Worlds! It *drinks* the stuff!"

"Did you," asked Blake softly, "say it would freeze?"

The tube dipped again, another monstrous beast joined the first. Two tremendous smacks resounded, bounced against the cliff behind them, and floated off. The first coiled up its huge, sucking tube again, and rolled blithely out of the lake towards the two men.

Blake ran clumsily, Penton close behind him. The huge cylinder chased down toward them at a speed of fully forty miles an hour, rolling like a mad barrel down hill. Madly, the two explorers raced for the deep, narrow crevice in the cliff wall, dived into it as the whole rocky wall jarred to the impact of the rolling brute.

Penton looked back. The crevice was stopped by a jetty flank, jammed against the rocky wall to a height of thirty feet.

"It can't get in, that's sure," he panted.

The flank retreated, jerking, heaving clumsily. It twisted, turned, scraped and bumped. Another huge cylinder came slamming along and bounced against it. Laboriously, the first continued its bouncing movements, now end-on to the crevice. The great, blunt end plugged the tiny crevice that sheltered the men.

Penton grunted.

"One at a time, gentlemen, one at a time," he said. "It won't do you any—for—jump!" The black leathery end split; the coiled, trunklike member was exposed, also a dozen twenty-foot long tentacular things that whipped out toward them. Penton jumped, Blake before him, back toward the dwindling, narrow end of the crevice. Too slow, the lashing tentacle caught Penton in a thrown noose of leathery strength; an immensely powerful, living rope snapped around his leg, tripped him, and yanked him back.

Jerked through the air helplessly, upside down, he was slammed against the black, wrinkled hide of the huge thing. Instantly, half a dozen tentacles snapped around and against him, forcing him against the black surface.

Supernal, dredging cold sucked the heat from his body. It was a numbing pressure that paralyzed him, forced him into the rubbery, yielding leather of the vast beast. His heat-pack could not offset the awful, unutterable chill of the vast bulk that had pressed him against itself. The blood roared in his ears as he struggled madly to free his arm, to get a chance to try the proton gun.

A flame of intolerable light burst abruptly somewhere near, a wash of momentary heat, gratefully warming. The huge, living ropes contracted spasmodically against him, but as he was already nearly buried in the blubbery monster's side, little added strain pressed against him. A vast ripple of muscles somewhere beneath the thick hide tossed him suddenly away from the body.

He stumbled dazedly to his feet. A slate-blue mass loomed near him. The ground beneath his feet was rumbling to the charge of half a dozen monsters rolling down toward the warm carcass. Staggering, the man rounded the flattening, squashing bulk, climbed over a nest of still-twitching ropes, and almost fell into the tiny crevice beyond.

"You're tougher than I thought." Blake grinned at his friend. "For a while I thought you were due for permanent residence here."

The dim light of the crevice faded yet further. A black hulk heaved and moved about on top of the cooling corpse at the mouth of the crevice. Penton looked up at it sadly.

"You might go get a dis gun, if you thought you could run fast, and throw those things out of your way. How were we to expect life here?

It isn't reasonable. Damn, brainless, mindless things that can't even be frightened."

"Not," said a very peculiar voice in his ears, "brainless. Merely that we have lost control," it added with a distinct note of sadness.

Blake looked slowly toward Penton. "Did you—"

Penton looked at Blake.

"Please," he asked softly, "don't be that way. You said that—"

"No," said the voice, "I did. I. I'm lying on top of Grugth here—the one you just killed."

Penton crawled farther back into the crevice, and looked back toward the mouth. Very dim against a black sky, the black beast bounced its way awkwardly over the hardening, slate-blue carcass.

"I'm sorry, you know," said the voice, plaintively, "but I can't help it. We evolved too far," it added in explanation.

"I hope you hear it, too," said Blake.

"Why? Misery loves company, or do you just want to make sure we're both crazy?" Penton looked unhappily at his friend. "I hear it, and I know I am. It comes right through the radio, and speaks English, which proves it."

"No, not at all. We can't speak by sound here; the air's too thin. On Earth, of course, animals developed sound-signaling. We developed radio, as you call it. I'm sorry if I disturb you. Would you rather I didn't speak? I would like to explain though, that it isn't maliciousness."

"Much," shuddered Blake. "Much rather you didn't speak. I'd rather die sane."

"No," said Penton. "You speak by radio, I can see how that might be, but *how* do you speak English?"

"Perhaps," said the voice apologetically, "Blake could shut off his receiver, if I disturb him. I hear you speaking, you see, and read minds, too, to a certain extent. I can't broadcast telepathy, but I do receive."

The black bulk heaved, and started to move uneasily.

"Oh, I'm sorry. I'm afraid I'm going away. Maybe one of the others will—"

The black wall of blubbery flesh heaved, humped, and rolled rapidly down. It vanished from their sight behind the other. They heard a new voice.

"Grugth," it said, "is cooling rapidly. I'm afraid I shan't be able to stay much longer. I'd like to, of course, but—" The voice faded as another creature rolled leisurely away.

"Are they, or are we nuts? We must be," stated Blake.

"I don't know," Penton replied hopelessly. "They've all gone away. Suppose we try sneaking over toward the ship."

Carefully Penton climbed over the frozen, dead thing. Fully two thousand of the immense things were grouped about the lake. Most of them were working at the bluish sand that circled the little pool. At one end the blunt cylinder had opened, and the familiar two-foot tube was sucking and smacking at the surface of the lake, drinking deep of the frightfully cold liquid.

The other end of each had also opened. A great, dark cavern had opened inside the protective outer covering of the blunt end, and a dozen ropy tentacles ending in broad, spatulate tips were busy shoveling the bluish, gritty, solid oxygen into the cavern.

"Maybe," said Penton thoughtfully, "we aren't crazy. I can see that, and that's no more possible than a brainless hulk like that learning English in about five minutes. It's eating solid oxygen at one end as fast as it can go, and drinking liquid hydrogen at the other, and with lamentable table manners, too. And except for those doing the same, or playing cuddle-pup with our ship, the whole blasted gang is lying out there sunning themselves in that ultra-dilute sunlight. They're all hanging around the ship, though."

"Sorry," interrupted a soft, slightly accented voice. "I'm afraid I'm coming. You'd better get back in the crevice."

Ted Penton looked and jumped. For all their immense bulk, their softness permitted them to move absolutely soundlessly. A hundred feet away, and coming rapidly, a huge bulk rolled along the cliff toward them. Together the two men jumped back into the cliff. The ground jarred to the impact of the thing as it smashed against the rock. By momentum it mounted its frozen brother.

"Ah," it remarked pleasantly, "I think I am going to stay—yes, yes, I am. But you had better move back a bit to safety." The thing was heaving and bouncing with an incredible awkwardness, trying to turn end on. "Apparently I am going to turn with my tentacles to reach you. If you will get well back, though, you'll be all right. There, I'm sure I'll stay a long time. This is fine."

The thing turned. Awkwardly, heavily, but it turned. Long, ropy tentacles reached vainly as the two men retreated as far as the dwindling crevice permitted.

"Fine," groaned Blake. "We want to get out of here."

"I know," sighed the creature. "But I really am as helpless as you are. I'd suggest you destroy me as you did Grugth, but it would do no good. The rest of them would come then."

"What," asked Penton, exasperation in his voice, "are you anyway? You are a brainless, awkward, sluggish bulk. You are the ultimate of mindless matter. But you learn English in minutes, you read minds, you sound intelligent."

"It is bewildering, isn't it? I'd like very much to help you, but I don't know just how. You see, originally we were intelligent creatures, well adapted to this inhospitable world."

"Inhospitable," groaned Blake, "is not an adequate word."

"But we're really very well adapted." The huge bulk heaved and struggled to drive itself into the impossibly narrow crevice. "I seem to be injuring myself trying to crawl in there. Really no sense at all, you see, in this stupid flesh. But it's a very cleverly designed body. The plains, you know. They stretch out for thousands of miles. These are practically the only mountains on the planet, as you may know—I see you do. And there is so little heat. Therefore, to a compact form like a cylinder, with no heat dissipating, narrow legs are advantageous. And, of course, the more bulk, the more volume in proportion to surface. That's why we are so big. Clumsy, of course, terribly awkward things. But we get along nicely on the plains. I do wish I'd stop trying to squeeze in there. I'm just injuring myself."

"Well, why in the name of space don't you?" Blake exploded.

"I can't, you see. I've evolved too much."

IV. EVOLUTION

Penton stared.

"Evolved too much?"

"Yes. Originally, as I say, we were fairly intelligent animals. This black skin, as you see, passes heat only one way, so we are not cold. We eat oxygen and drink hydrogen, and eat a few other things. Occasionally a *drutheg*. That's one of those round things you thought were boulders. And we sun ourselves."

"What is a *drutheg*?"

"It's—let me see—oh, yes. A sort of plant. It moves around very, very slowly, staying near streams and lakes. Most of them live in streams. They consume water, and nitrogen, and some other things, and sun themselves, and throw out oxygen and hydrogen. There is practically no water on this entire planet; the *drutheg* break it all down to hydrogen and oxygen. All the water there is, is in our bodies; we make it, you understand, from the food we eat."

"But," protested Blake, "that doesn't explain how you come to say you wish you'd stop trying to get in here, but go right on trying."

"As I say, we started as fairly intelligent animals, living on heat and oxygen and hydrogen, but we had to spend all our time, practically, seeking those things. So gradually we developed the ability to think our thoughts while the body took care of itself. You—yes, I see you can walk along while reading a magazine or book. Your mind sort of leaves the body to look after itself for a while. We developed the trick. It took me nearly two hundred years practice—our years—"

"Two hundred of *your* years! That's over 80,000 Earth-years!"

"Yes. Those inner planets do go around the sun at a crazy pace, don't they? As I say—oh, length of life? Well, practically nothing can kill us here on this world and nothing bothers us. We live very peaceful lives, normally. In fact, it is terribly hard to get rid of one's self. We normally live about three thousand years, about a million and a quarter of your years. I'm about a million."

Blake looked at the creature. Black, blunt-ended cylinder, squirming tentacles stretched out to reach them. A million years—

"But I learned the trick, and learned it so well that I spent years on end without paying the slightest attention to my body. Of course, in that time we had developed our language to a considerable extent, and our thoughts. We had deduced nearly all the basic facts concerning space, and began to see the advantages of mechanisms. We were drawing up plans to build a spaceship to visit other worlds in person."

The voice sighed, very sorrowfully. "Then we found our bodies had learned a trick, too. It had been nearly a thousand years since any of us had paid any attention to our bodies. Occasionally it had been annoying to have our bodies roll away from someone we were talking to in order to find food. But now we decided to go to work again. And then we made the sad discovery."

The voice deepened mournfully.

"We had forgotten our bodies so long that they had been forced to develop a certain amount of mental equipment. A sort of secondary mind. They had minds of their own, and we can't control them any more."

Blake gasped. "Can't—control—them—any more?"

"No. Apparently the nerve-channels connecting the intellectual portion of our minds with the purely physical parts have atrophied. Not one of us has the slightest control. I couldn't be staying here if it weren't that my body feels the heat you radiate and stupidly keeps trying to reach it."

"How," asked Penton, "does that one-way heat transfer of yours work? I'd like to have something like that."

"It works only at low temperatures, with living tissue," the voice explained. "And I can't tell you in your language, and you haven't time to learn mine. We can't control our bodies, but I notice you can't control all your minds either."

"Huh? What do you mean?" asked Blake in surprise.

"Part of your mind is very worried, and very busy trying to find a way to get out of that crack in the cliff. It is particularly worried since it took note of a small click that represented the change from the first to the spare oxygen tank. But you don't seem to be aware of it with your conscious mind."

Blake glanced down. A small gauge in his helmet definitely agreed with the creature. Tank 2 was being exhausted slowly but steadily. Simultaneously, almost, Penton did hear, consciously, the click that meant his tank-mechanism had switched. One oxygen bottle was exhausted.

"Were those full?" Penton asked Blake quizzically.

Blake nodded dumbly. "Two hours—"

"They should have gone three," Penton pointed out.

"May I help? Your subconscious has already figured it out. This world is heavier, you've been working unusually hard, and all your muscles have to maintain a higher tonic property. They are consuming an unusually large quantity of oxygen. You timed those bottles, I take it, on your moon? Gravity was light there, and your requirements much lower."

"That is the answer, but it doesn't get us more oxygen."

"You have also been wondering about that solid oxygen on the floor. You might try it," the voice suggested.

Blake looked down. Bluish, sandy crystals of oxygen swept in by faint winds littered the floor, mingled with tiny particles of rock dust and nitrogen.

"We can try."

Penton unstrapped Blake's tank. Together they swept up the oxygen crystals and poured them into the cylinder's mouth. Nearly five minutes were required to warm them through liquid to gas; then the tank mechanism in Blake's helmet snapped.

Instantly his hands clawed at the valves, turning them down, switching back to the original. "Phew—it smells. You can't breathe that frightful stuff."

"Oxygen," said the voice sadly, "used to have a very pleasant and distinctive flavor, varying with the type of *drutheg* that produced it. We never taste it any more. We don't even feel the pleasantness of heat any more. And heat was a very pleasant sensation."

"So," sighed Penton, "I notice. That gang around our ship—"

"They are very sorry, but there's nothing at all they can do. They don't have control, you see. Ah—look. I do believe I've seriously injured myself at last."

The tentacles writhed back, the leathery protective membrane snapped back over the cylinder's blunt end, but not completely. The monstrous thing had succeeded in jamming itself into the crevice to a considerable extent, and a sudden wriggle had brought an abrupt collapse of one side of the thing.

A thick, gummy substance was spurting out, to harden instantly as it touched the frightfully chilled rock. "I think," said the voice with an air of pleased surprise, "that I've finally succeeded in killing myself."

"Succeeded—you sound pleased!" Penton stared at the huge thing, flopping erratically now, struggling to get free once more.

"Naturally—oh yes. The bone was broken and it's pierced a main blood vessel. That should take about ten minutes. Wouldn't you be pleased to get free of this stupid, useless lump of awkward flesh? Naturally I'm pleased. I know Grugth was immensely satisfied when he succeeded in setting up his force-pattern, after nearly twenty-seven hundred years."

"What," asked Blake, "is a force-pattern?"

"I can't quite explain," the voice said rather hurriedly. "I haven't much time. I'll have to start setting up mine. And anyway, your language is strictly limited. I have been working out the basic structure of my pattern for nearly 1,000,000 of your years. Do not mistake; my mentality compares with yours only when speaking your language. I have spent over one million of your years in unending thought and study. I could solve any problem for you—instruct you in making the weapon you need, or in generating pure force-fields to return you to your home planet, had either your language or your brain the necessary capacity.

"But I must leave you, for this flesh of mine is going rapidly. Good-bye. I believe your subconscious has a solution to—no—water—water—" The voice stopped. A slate-blue tinge crept out from the wounded side of the monster. Slowly, the immense bulk flattened down, the muscular tension that had held it in a round, powerful figure was dying. Loggedly it rolled off the cold, dead thing beneath it. The ground shook faintly with the hurried coming of others of the Titan beasts. Coming to feast on the heat escaping from the carcass.

"I think," said Penton softly, "I begin to get it. Mindless flesh, and super-minds, super-minds imprisoned in stupid things. Stupid bodies, however, cleverly designed by the neverending plans of Nature to survive on this incredibly inhospitable world. Their leathery hide is black because it absorbs all light, all energy that strikes it, and converts it to heat. There's darned little heat, but what there is they absorb, and won't let out. By accumulation, they end up with a very considerable supply. With death, that membrane passes heat both ways, that is, the stored heat escapes. They are, by purely involuntary reaction, attracted toward any source of heat, of course, so they absorb the heat of the dead bulk, as they seek our heat, and the heat of the ship. Quite involuntarily."

"Quite, I assure you," added a new voice. "I'm sorry your weapon is so nearly exhausted. The fuel-wires are almost spent?"

"About three shots left in each, I guess." Blake agreed sorrowfully. "They weren't intended as weapons. We didn't expect any life here."

"There's life on every planet of the System," the speaker assured them. "You will meet most of the important forms."

"Could you tell me how to fix these proton projectors so they'll fire a few more shots? That might give us a better chance to see those other forms of life," Blake suggested bitterly.

"Sorry. Your language isn't up to it. If I could control your bodies, or my own, I might be able to do it. But if I could control my body, you wouldn't need them fixed, and I'd have made up my force-pattern ages ago."

"What is this force-pattern?" Penton demanded. "The last one of you who spoke to us mentioned it."

"At the instant of death, the mind, the pure mentality is released. Thought has power: the fact that one mind can influence another indicates that. If properly managed at the moment of death, a vortex in space can be made, and the vortex is stable through eternity, unless the mind desires to break it down. It is utterly free to propel itself where it wills. Stray energies of space give it power if it chooses to increase its intensity. But it can be achieved only by the dissolution of the physical brain.

"And," the voice was bitterly sorrowful, "I can't control this stupid bulk long enough to destroy it. Any of us would gladly aid you back to your ship if only you would destroy these masses of flesh and release us."

"The only masses of flesh that stand any chance of destruction," Penton pointed out, "are our own. And we are not at all anxious to lose them."

"I know. I am sorry. I'm afraid—I am going." The ground shook slightly. Three immense cylinders rolled awkwardly away across the plain, to feed at the margin of the little lake. Faintly, a warning came back.

"If you step out, I'll have to come back. I—" The voice faded beyond the power of the transceivers.

V. EXAMPLE

"What in blazes are we going to do?" Blake demanded. "They are friendly, they're brilliant, no doubt, but they're still stupid, brainless, annihilating Juggernauts."

"Blazes," said Penton softly. "What in blazes. In blazes, of course." He laughed. "Stupid of me. Remarkably."

Blake looked at him silently. Then: "I'm stupider. What about blazes?"

"Hydrogen," said Penton, "a river and a lake of hydrogen. A lake of hydrogen with a beach of solid oxygen. 'Water' was what the one called just before he set up—his force-pattern. They want to die; well, by the gods of space, they will. They have to go toward heat, whether they like it or not. Hydrogen and oxygen make water—and a hell of a lot of heat."

"Oh," said Blake softly. "So they do." He looked out of their little crevice. Thirty feet away the little stream of liquid hydrogen crept through little islands of solid oxygen.

Penton climbed up on the bulk of the dead, frozen monsters, leveled his proton projector at the rim of the little stream, and pressed the button. A fierce, flaming spot of incandescence exploded both into their primal gases, swirled them violently. Licking lightnings spun and shattered on other crystals and liquid drops.

And the heat died. Two huge cylinders started rolling, but stopped as the last trace of heat vanished. Liquid hydrogen rained back from the air, solid oxygen snowed down.

Penton stared.

"Blake, it didn't burn!"

Blake looked blankly at his friend.

"It just has to. The laws of chemistry can't be that different. That must have been a freak—a chance, because the stuff is so cold out here. Try again."

And, Penton shot the flaming energy of the protons crashing into the margin, where hydrogen lapped against the solid oxygen. Again, the explosive rush of solid and liquid abruptly converted into gas—and again it settled as liquid rain and solid snow.

Penton looked at his friend, and shrugged his shoulders.

"New laws of chemistry, I guess. They won't burn. That's out."

Blake sighed.

"My oxygen tank is getting low. And the valves aren't working right. I had to fuss with them several times. Guess I jammed them when I tried to turn off that damned odor. Maybe that smelly stuff is some kind of catalyst that prevents combustion."

Slowly he turned up the oxygen valve, cursing fluently.

"The valve stuck again, and I nearly passed out. It would have made a lot of difference, wouldn't it?"

"Not much that I can see," admitted Penton. "No weapons. No way to hide. We can't wait until they just wander away. No way of restoring our oxygen. No way of reaching the ship."

Blake only growled and turned up his oxygen a bit. Slowly he got to his feet, his panting stopped by the renewal of the oxygen supply. He walked over toward the dead things, climbed up on the lower one to look across the plain. Near at hand, the stubborn stream of hydrogen twisted through new channels between the blasted pits where Penton's protons had exploded shore and stream alike into gas.

Blake reeled slightly.

"Stupid," he muttered. "Shtupid beassh. Stupid hydroshen, stupid oxyshen. Won' burn. Here, shtupid, water. Make thish shtuff." Blake was gloriously drunk; his oxygen control was stuck again, wide open, and he was thoroughly intoxicated by the excess oxygen. Penton looked up and climbed hastily toward him as he unscrewed the water bottle from his spacesuit, and hurled it out toward the stream. "There, shtupid hydroshen, make 'at shtuff." He raised his proton gun waveringly, and pressed the button.

The explosion sent him flying backward, crashed him into Penton, and sent both tumbling back into the crevice. An immense, mile-high jet of blue flame licked roaring into the black sky, a finger of fire that reached to the stars. The tiny stream of hydrogen vanished in the fiery heat, the oxygen melted, boiled, hissed into shrilling flame. A darting line of flame licked along the brink of the lake, consuming oxygen sand and hydrogen water alike, shouting and howling. In seventeen seconds the lake was ringed by flame, the hydrogen-fall was a cloud of ascending gas.

Two thousand bulks were joyfully, thunderously flinging themselves into the mighty pyre, to explode in sudden death as their tissues boiled. Thundering down slopes to that heat, the brainless bodies reacted only to an instinctive search for heat; never had they met killing heat.

Penton clamped down Blake's oxygen valve, and heaved him to his feet, starting him running. The flames were half a mile away now, a vast circle of fire reaching to the skies. There was neither oxygen sand, nor hydrogen stream here. At the point where it left the lake, the stream was flowing upward as flaming gas. Only bare, faintly warm rock lay exposed. Blake straightened before they had gone a hundred feet, shook his head and opened his valve slightly.

"Oxy-drunk. My God, what happened?"

"Shut up and move," Penton grunted. "Turn the oxygen a little high, but don't get drunk again. We have to get to the ship before that fire goes out completely. It's almost a mile."

Burdened by their greater weight, they plugged along as best they could. Presently, they arrived at the ship. Penton carried him into the lock, and slammed the great door shut.

"What happened?" gasped Blake weakly, as he opened his eyes.

"Water." Penton grinned. "Water—just as we were warned. It needed a sample, just as you gave it. Hydrogen and oxygen will not unite in the total absence of water. It's old, but I never thought of it. And all those *drutheg* working and reworking that stuff for that last, ultimate trace of water. It wouldn't burn until your water bottle supplied that trace it needed to start. Let's move into the ship, and clear out for warmer planets."

THE BRAIN PIRATES

I. DOUBLE GRAVITY

The *Ion* propelled itself powerfully through the void. Inside the craft, Rodney Blake's arm reached out in a dramatic gesture of disclosure. Half a hundred thousand miles away hung a dusty, underripe peach. It was dim and hard to see, here, where the sun's light was diluted by five billion miles of space.

"There she is, skipper," he told his permanent partner, Ted Penton. "The only satellite of the Tenth World! Are we still going to investigate it?"

"We sure are. As long as we are this far out from the sun, we may as well see what's seeable," Penton answered firmly. "We have those new suits rigged with atomic-powered lifting gadgets, so that'll protect us from the weight, if what our instruments say about that world's true. I still don't see how any member of this System could be so confoundedly dense. This satellite has a diameter of thirty-four hundred miles, yet the surface gravity is double that of Earth!"

Blake whistled softly.

"Incidentally," he said, "we ought to land in about half an hour. Any suggestions as to where to go? Try your telescope."

Penton disappeared into the observatory booth and came back presently with a rough-sketch map.

"I was up there just before I slept. That was nine hours ago, and this place here on the sketch was in the nightshade then, glowing faintly. I think it may be a highly radioactive section. Looking through the 'scope just now, I see it has moved into daylight, and the glow is hidden by the sunlight, weak as it is out here, but there is some funny, rainbow colored mineral formation there. Let's land there. I'll go check up on those suits, and make some adjustments. I hadn't thought they'd have to handle any double-gravity worlds."

"That's a swell map," complained Blake. "You've drawn the thing from the image in an astronomical 'scope. It's inverted. I'm going to be too busy to figure out mirror images. And may I suggest that you make sure you don't get those drive-units in the suits backward? I'd hate to have them sit on me as well as a doubled gravity."

Penton grinned and went down the corridor toward the airlock, picking up a kit of tools from the machine-shop bench as he passed. Presently he was deeply engrossed in the delicate task of readjusting the tiny atomic-power drive-units he had fixed in the spacesuits. The mobility these would furnish would have been highly welcome at the time they had been visiting the Tenth World.

"Oh, Ted!" Penton raised his head abruptly from the work of fastening down the cover plate that engaged his attention for the past twenty minutes. The slightly metallic voice had issued from the airlock speaker over his head.

"Yes?"

"We're about to land," said Blake's voice. "Help take over. Throw the switch. And I hope those suits suit us!"

* * * *

Penton and Blake stared fretfully through the windows of the *Ion*. The inhabitants of the satellite were regarding the explorers with a mild curiosity.

"Those birds are waiting with remarkable patience," Penton said, somewhat annoyed. "And this seems to be the local Central Park, wherefore our landing may have annoyed them. Come on, you have a UV gun on one hip, and a disintegrator on the other, and—"

"Lead in both legs. Did you notice that local yokel to the left of us make a slow, stately bow? He snapped like a flag in the wind. I'll bet they can move five times as fast as we can—or at least two times as fast. This gravity's faster."

"Not faster than 186,000 miles a second," Penton declared firmly. "Did you observe them closely? Mount one olive on one grapefruit. Two fat sausages protruding from the opposite sides of said grapefruit just below the olive, two fatter frankfurters at the nether end, all add up to equal one—Tenthworldsatelliteian."

"They do have a chubby air"—Blake grinned—"but I don't claim to move 186,000 miles a second. And these boys do move fast."

"They're patient anyway, much more so than I am. Lift your blasted carcass and come on. They're a pretty human looking gang, even if they do look like prize-winners in the Fat Men's Club. Besides, fat men are always jolly. You know as well as I do that you're coming in the end, so let's go."

Reluctantly Blake heaved. He heaved harder, remaining curiously fixed to his seat.

"Boy, am I agile," he grunted softly, and gave in. Slowly he turned up the lift-control at his belt. A slow creaking of straps and an unhappy wriggling on Blake's part attested to the increasing power of the atomic drive mounted on the suit. Blake rose. "I can't even stand up without the aid of this thing. Let's go."

Penton opened the outer lock door. Blake stepped down, or better, floated down behind Penton. The gravity-equalizer made him feel as if he were riding on a parachute. Penton faced the strange inhabitants and slowly raised both hands above his head in a gesture of friendship.

He'd intended to hold them out horizontally in front of him, but the effort, under that gravity, was distinctly uncomfortable.

"From a much lighter world, aren't you?" suggested a rather philosophically friendly telepathic voice. "From an inner planet? Well—I have always been convinced there were more than five inner planets."

"Ten," said Penton automatically. "We're from the third."

One of the immensely rounded inhabitants of this world nodded in pleased acknowledgement.

"Ah, interesting. Very. The third world, then, and there are twelve."

"Twelve?"

Blake stared at the moon-faced spokesman.

"Oh, so, so. Ah, yes. Two more. That makes twelve. That's even more interesting. There are two worlds further out. Remarkably small eyes you have, if I may say so. The bright light near the sun, I suppose."

Blake nodded vaguely. The moon-faced inhabitant did have large eyes; it was only the immense roundness of his face that made them appear small. Now at the ground level, Blake could better judge their height and size. About five feet tall, each was, and approximately six feet in circumference at the equator—which was quite marked. They resembled diminutive, but well inflated carnival balloons made in caricature shapes.

"It looks," said Penton softly, "as though we'll have to go way out before we go back toward the sun. We'll have to see those two worlds."

"Yes, see them. Interesting ship you have. We've been trying for some time to make one like it—atomic power, eh? Yes. Will you accompany us?... I, by the way, am Terruns, associated with the Power and Mechanisms Department of Runal City. Oh, this world? We call our primary, Turlun, and our satellite here is called Pornan.

"But I think we may go to the city. The members of the Power and Mechanisms Department have been very anxious to speak with you since your ship was first sighted. There was rather a flurry there as to where you would land. Very proud to have you in our city. You will come? Our cars are ahead."

"Why—yes," said Penton, slightly bewildered. Then, more firmly, "Yes, we will be very interested to see more of your civilization on this world so far from the sun. Our lives, our civilization, you understand, are all based on the movements or apparent movements of the sun."

Terruns waved briskly in a vertical plane. His remarkably rotund body did not crease, so far as Blake's closely watching, interested eye could determine, but simply contracted vertically, and spread laterally in front, with a reversal of this process in back. The queerly hectic bowing of the comically grapefruitish body fascinated Blake, with the same childish wonder that the incomprehensible leg-work of the millipede inspires.

Terruns straightened abruptly and regarded Penton closely with large, dark eyes.

"The ship, by the way. It does not move in your absence?" he asked, somewhat anxiously.

Penton looked at him somewhat blankly.

"No, it is manually controlled—it will stay where it is."

The round face parted in a somewhat fatuous smile of satisfaction.

"Ah, excellent. Yes, if it stays there, that will be well. You will know it is here. Come with us. Yes, a lighter world. The supports in the suits—very ingenious, very—" His mental speech faded off gradually. Blake and Penton watched with interest as the dozen or so Pornans set off in perfect unison across the close-cropped turf. Each was dressed in a precisely uniform outfit of apparently skin-tight elastic fabric, of a rather pleasing, greenish hue in itself, but covered with a repetitive and complex pattern of spirals and sharp-angled zigzags.

The Pornans' legs were rather short, and distinctly over the "stout" classification. But they worked like frantic pumps, bouncing up and down at a flurried pace, while the associated body rocked and rolled in a manner curiously reminiscent of a round-bodied bell-buoy in a choppy sea. But they made progress, such progress, considering their girth, that for a moment, Blake and Penton stood in astonished surprise, while their guides almost disappeared over a little pink swale of land.

"Did you notice the turf?" Penton asked Blake as they followed behind. "It's apparently a sort of moss, and a remarkably pink one at that. But then, the trees are, too. Incidentally, they don't use sunlight as a source of energy, of course. Look, our hosts seem to have arrived at their car."

A moment later, Penton and Blake had arrived also. There were, accurately, three cars. They were very commodious cars, until the Pornans climbed in. They accomplished that act with a surprising ease and actual grace, despite their immense girth. The cars themselves were merely open platforms, in effect, seating six Pornans in three cross seats, two to a seat. Each place was equipped with a very solidly made rail, on which the passengers immediately placed both feet. Their hands settled comfortably, and firmly into handgrips in their seat-arms.

Four wheels, scarcely eighteen inches in diameter, and consisting exclusively of pneumatic tires supported the vehicle. A small square case behind the rearmost seat, contained the engine; from the size of its case, it was a wholly inadequate engine. But the two explorers clambered in.

"Hold fast," said Terruns cheerily. "It's only about a fifteen minute ride." Curiously, the time-designation was quite clear to the Terrestrials.

II. THE INVISIBLE CAR

Terruns stabbed viciously at a red button on the panel that formed the front of the car. Something in the box at the rear muttered faintly, and began throbbing furiously. Rapidly, from the sides, a pinkish mass protruded, until, inside of ten seconds, a pneumatic bumper fully two feet thick had pushed out all about, front, side and rear.

"We're going," said their guide cheerfully, "to the center of the city. Power and Mechanisms Building, where all our broadcast energy is developed."

Blake understood suddenly the purpose of the rails and handgrips. The motor, whatever it was, was far from inadequate. The car moved to speed with a rush that snapped his head back viciously.

"We power nearly everything," continued Terruns, "by broadcast energy. Source of energy's the trouble. Very troublesome, because it's a frightful job concentrating the radioactive ores. Lasts a good while, but power demands growing faster than ore-concentrate available. Perhaps—"

Blake closed his eyes and held on as Terruns sailed blithely toward the side of another car coming out of a side street. Abruptly he was hurled from his seat, and draped over Terruns' immense shoulders. The Pornan yielded softly under him, but not sufficiently to cushion the violent shock. Blake opened his eyes to observe the details of the collision, and saw Terruns' head turned completely around on an amazingly flexible neck, regarding him in faint surprise.

"Ah, yes, light worlds. So. So sorry. I'll slow down more gently." The head pivoted outrageously, and the car jerked forward, depositing Blake in his seat once more.

"Penton," said Blake softly, bracing himself solidly, "can you find the way back? I want to walk." He closed his eyes again, for they had left the roadways of the park and entered the heavy, city traffic. It was, quite evidently, suicidally inclined, or else controlled solely by inspired maniacs.

Somewhere in the depths of his mind, the thought popped that here, evidently, the movies got those impossible scenes of a mad ride through New York traffic at impossible speed. Not that the cars moved rapidly. At their best, in fact, Terruns had maintained no better than twenty miles an hour; but the utter indifference to safety, the half-inch margins gleefully accepted by the drivers made that insane reckless- ness.

The purpose of the huge bumpers inflated about them seeped into Blake's mind. His eyes refused to close again, because he wanted to know which way to jump. A brilliantly green vehicle tore down from a side street, swinging toward their rear as it appeared that they were to escape, then braked violently to permit them to move out of the way by a fraction of an inch.

"Traffic," said Terruns somewhat annoyedly, "always disturbs me. How do they control traffic in your world?"

"The problem is worse," said Penton through clenched teeth, "though less disturbing to us." He paused to grip violently and brace himself as Terruns braked the car to a dead stop in a distance that did not exist. "Traffic lights—not so disturbing to us, because braking—"

"Ah, yes. Very difficult on light world." Traffic moved again, jumping forward as though seen on a broken film, inexpertly patched. They were in motion. "The traction is much less, on a lighter world, is it not? The inertia to mass to weight ratio—"

Blake looked around with a sudden relief. He had been too startled and frightened to think. On this world, where great weight forced their tires solidly into the greenish glasslike pavement, brakes were infinitely more efficient, and—

They took a right-angle corner with an abruptness that had him half out of the car, his feet on the thick, pneumatic bumper before he gripped the rail and pulled himself in again. And—cars gripped better on turns. The mad driving was comparatively sane on that basis.

"I have no patience with some drivers we have," Terruns told them. "Reckless. Use no judgment, and show no respect for other people." No sooner had he said this when he halted his vehicle a sickening half an inch from the bumper of the car ahead.

"Relative," said Penton softly. "All things are relative—especially speed and acceleration," and he gripped the rail in preparation for the next start.

The road narrowed, became a two-lane street. Blake was recovering, as the better understanding of local conditions penetrated. Suddenly there was a violent explosion from the empty air directly ahead of them, a flash of violet flame, and white smoke. Instantly Terruns jammed on the brakes, and a violent thud of pneumatic bumpers crashed the car to a halt so short that Penton and Blake both sailed into the air.

They sailed along for some hundreds of feet through the air before descending, their lifting units now advanced to support them entirely. A series of popping explosions like a string of firecrackers sounded behind them, and a howl like a dog whose paw has been stepped on followed and accompanied.

Together the Terrestrials looked back. Terruns and his followers were looking at them in mild bewilderment. Its great bumper hard against that of the machine they had so recently quitted, a similar vehicle carrying two Pornans occupied the formerly vacant volume of air. These also were watching the Terrestrials with interest.

"I think I know," said Penton in slow disgust, "why they go only twenty miles an hour. Will you tell me what in hell is the idea of driving around in an invisible car? Or is that the police system here? If it is, I consider it notably screwier than even this wabble-eyed planet. Great Wavering Worlds!"

Terruns nodded toward them with evident relief on his face.

"Remarkable—very remarkable, your flight. For a moment I feared you might land rather heavily—but why didn't you just hold on? We usually do." For a man of his girth, he displayed a surprising ease in the agile jump that carried him over the enormous bumper to the roadway. The driver of the other car jumped down to meet him, and the two bowed jerkily in perfect unison. Together they walked to the point of collision.

The two cars nuzzled each other like amorous hippopotamuses. Terruns inspected the front of his machine as Penton and Blake approached, Penton's mouth somewhat angular.

"No damage?" suggested the driver of the second car.

Terruns beamed cheerfully.

"No damage," he agreed.

The second driver swung nimbly into his seat, nodded good-bye. His car swerved violently backward, braked, then swung forward and away with a savage acceleration.

"Is it customary to drive around in invisible cars?" interrupted Penton plaintively. "I should think it would make traffic more than a little confusing."

"Sorry, my friend. Very unusual now. But no damage, no damage at all. In the last six months, but two people have been killed in such collisions." Terruns looked rather proudly at the enormous inflated sausage that circled the car. "Some of my men developed that. Very effective—very simple."

"Excellent, no doubt. But why have invisible cars in the first place? You were, I assure you, no less surprised than we that we did not land heavily. And how do you accomplish that invisibility?"

Terruns sighed.

"Not by choice. We don't accomplish it. Look. Come—" Terruns started forward to meet the slowly approaching Terrestrials. Suddenly his immense body seemed to tangle in his feet, and he fell with a resounding crash. The force of the impact dented his pudgy body by several inches, and for a moment he lay there, rather startled eyes slowly winking. A queerly mischievous, chuckling gurgle came from the empty air beside him, and it seemed to Penton that a sort of vertical heat wave in the air danced down the street, to vanish as suddenly as it had come into being.

Terruns' large eyes blinked once more, and he shook his head. He rose to his feet with a sigh of annoyance, just as one of the hurrying Pornans from the rear of the car reached him.

"Damn *krull*," he exclaimed. The frown faded from his moon face and his usual good-natured philosophy seemed to rule again. "Unusually persistent, wasn't he? I suppose he has gone. Ah, well. I could smell singed hair. I hope he learned something."

Blake stared at him in considerable wonder.

"What is a *krull*?" he asked.

For once, Terruns did not reply immediately. He looked thoughtfully at Blake, and even more thoughtfully at Penton.

"Monkey," he said at length. "Ape—no, monkey." Then he nodded, smiling somewhat vaguely. "A *krull* is somewhat like your monkey. A higher species. Quite intelligent. Delights in mischief. Smaller than we are, and very bony. Oh, very." Terruns rubbed his pudgy leg vigorously, the soft flesh denting deeply under his fingers.

"Are they—invisible?" Blake looked about him vaguely. "I gathered you had tripped over one, but unless they are a good deal smaller than you, I don't see how I missed it."

Terruns nodded sadly.

"They disrupt economic life. Mischievous, just mischievous. And they love excitement. When we first started using automobiles they caused no end of excitement. All our higher species have telepathic powers. *Krulls*, very sad, have great powers. Not intelligent, not quite reasoning, perhaps, but almost. And remarkable vision. Eyes unlike ours. One on each side of the head like—oh, your rabbit? Rabbits see in all directions also? Yes, so do *krulls*. And telepathic, marvelously so. That makes them invisible."

Penton looked at the Pornan thoughtfully for a moment.

"Sorry, my friend, you have skipped a step somewhere. How does that make them invisible?"

"Well, now see. You see me. Now—" Terruns grinned and wasn't there.

III. THE STOLEN SHIP

Penton wiggled his head slowly, and looked more carefully. Definitely there was a large, and conspicuous hole in the landscape, a large, grayish mist that swirled and seethed with a curious riot of colors and angles and impossibly shaped buildings.

Abruptly Terruns was back. Blake looked at him with considerable distaste.

"Can all of you do that?"

"It's very simple," nodded Terruns. "But we can't see a *krull*. I merely telepathized the idea that I wasn't there. Momentarily you were deceived, but quickly reasoned that I *must* be there, because of the hole in the landscape. Therefore you saw me again. A *krull*, of course, sees in all directions, and therefore can fill the hole in the landscape by telepathizing two things. He isn't there. You see the landscape. Very simple."

Blake looked at Penton from the side of his eyes.

"Ted, shall we go for a walk? Back to the ship, maybe. Somehow telepathizing imps don't promise well."

"They make themselves completely invisible in that way?" asked Penton.

"Quite," Terruns replied. A more serious expression crossed his face as he explained further the troubles of his people. "And worse, as you saw. They make automobiles invisible. Sit on the bumper in front. They like excitement and that sometimes makes a lot of excitement." His face lighted a bit as he nodded toward the car. "But not so much since the fire-vents were installed."

"Oh. Explosives?"

"Yes. Serves two purposes. First, if I see a car coming toward me that doesn't seem to see me, I know a *krull* is riding in front. I press a button on the panel. Explosions warn the other driver, and we both brake sharply. Also explosions immediately under *krull* usually induce them to move. Frequently the *krull* gets caught between cars, which is very good. Usually," he sighed, "they escape, merely somewhat singed. But they are intelligent. They learn."

"Why the devil don't you drive them away?"

Terruns smiled sadly.

"How? We would very much like to. Oh, no end. But no results. They steal our food, they steal anything that will move. Don't attack us, because we are very much stronger. Very hard to shoot what you can't see."

"Great Worlds, Terruns, can't you get rid of the creatures somehow? Use colored glasses so you see differently than they, and make them visible. Any trick like that?"

"Trick? Oh, my dear friend, the mind is tricked. It does no good to trick our eyes, when our minds are tricked. We have tried a truly remarkable assortment of mechanisms," Terruns sighed, "but none of them work."

"From your fall, I should think people would be very badly injured tripping over the blamed things," Blake suggested.

"That's why we wear these suits," Terruns replied.

"Suits?"

The moon face split in a good-natured grin.

"I'm not quite as large as this. It's the protective suit. It bounces." The Pornan touched something somewhere in his suit. Rapidly the seemingly skin-tight suit shrank. It hung in folds, disconsolate droops and lumps all over him. Then the elasticity of the suit began to work, and slowly it crawled back to a skin-tight fit in fact.

* * * *

An utterly different Terruns emerged. His body was squat and enormously powerful, the huge chest heavily banded with thick sheets and cords of muscle, great rippling cords of it flowing into thick, muscle-ridged arms. His torso tapered to a narrow waist, then expanded into blocky, corded legs. Far from pudgy, there was not an ounce of fat on that perfect specimen of the powerfully muscled denizen of this heavy-gravity world.

And with that alteration, his face seemed now subtly changed. The roundness was not the fullness of fat, but a roundness of differently shaped bones, and differently placed muscle-cords. The roundness differed from a human face as a bulldog's round face from the lean jaws of the wolfhound.

Blake whistled softly.

The Pornan's good-natured smile reappeared.

"Different worlds—different people."

"Different worlds," repeated Penton with a gentle moan, "different people. I, Blake, am different for life."

"Do you still remember that—six long hours ago? Old Elephant Penton. Can you remember anything else that was said?"

"Little." Penton moved gingerly. The motion, inasmuch as he was floating in Terruns' saltwater-filled swimming pod, sent his nose under the surface. He straightened out with hasty caution and a soft, but heartfelt remark. "Damn little. Six hours under doubled gravity and—" He stopped and looked up. Terruns was standing on the edge of the pool looking down at them with sad reproof.

"I asked you," their host said reproachfully, "I asked you particularly, but you said the ship would not move if you weren't there."

"Right," agreed Penton, paddling gently to bring himself to a vertical position. "You asked, and it won't."

"Sorry." Terruns shook his head. "Report from the Park Department. They can't find it. They didn't expect to see it. We never see things like that, but they can't feel it. Very unusual, if it can't be moved."

"What? Can't find our ship?"

"You said," Terruns began. He stopped abruptly as he leaped violently and awkwardly into the air, to land in the pool with a mighty thunder, and a tidal wave that all but swamped the Terrestrials. Immediately, the inflated suit brought him bobbing to the surface, lying on his stomach, his arms moving uselessly because of the airtight suit. They would not grip the water. Simultaneously there was a chuckling chatter and a loud *thump*.

Terruns released a mighty "oof" and sank six inches into the water. The chattering went on excitedly from empty air, while a mad splashing began on both sides of the balloonclad Pornan, as though an invisible side-wheeler in a frightful hurry had gone slightly askew. Terruns was gasping heavily, half stunned, while his body began to move in hurried circles to the accompaniment of much chattering.

Blake and Penton stared in paralyzed astonishment. Terruns recovered his wind, reached the tab on his suit, and Pornan and invisible rider plunged into the water. Instantly both struck out for the shore, and the *krull*, too busy otherwise to remain invisible, appeared.

A rabbit-eared, rabbit-faced, four-limbed creature the size of a ten-year-old child, it had a surprisingly chunky body. Details of arms and legs were rather blurred, as both were working with a truly amazing determination and efficiency. For a moment Terruns was handicapped as his suit shrank back to fit; then he too got into action. Arms churning like twin propellers and both feet going in a white froth of water, he overhauled the shrieking *krull*, a six-inch bow wave curling about his ears.

The little creature bounced out of the water when it reached the pool edge, and disappeared the instant it hit the tiled floor. Immediately behind it, Terruns swarmed up the lip of the pool and set off down the tile like a bloodhound on the trail. The wet animal was dripping revealingly. Halfway to the arched door at the far end, he skidded to a halt, and grabbed at the air. A yowling shriek greeted his move, and triumphantly he raised his arm. The shrieks continued but nothing appeared as a source.

Terruns walked back toward the pool more leisurely.

"You said," went on the Pornan calmly, "that it couldn't be moved, but it was. It isn't there." He reached the edge of the pool, and bent down. The shrieking chatter mounted; as he lowered his hand a hole appeared in the water, then a white froth. "Presently, my friends, I shall show you a *krull*. Very reckless fellow. They love to go paddling, though." The shrieking chatter had changed to an unhappy glubbing and a thunder of splashing water. Slowly the glubbing and splashing reached a climax and died away. The pool-edge, the water, and even Terruns wavered and twisted crazily in appearance. Then a wet, feebly kicking, half-drowned creature appeared, about six inches below the surface of the water.

"Oh," said Penton distastefully, "we have 'em on our world, too. They appear and disappear, and sometimes only one person can see them."

"Sure," said Penton. "We have a drug that makes them visible. Alcohol. We call them D.T.'s."

"Deetees," said Terruns mildly, looking down at the wet, slowly reviving creature. "Curious." The *krull's* rabbit ears drooped dejectedly, bright green rabbit ears drooping over a bright red face. The red faded gradually into a handsome purple body, marked by a large and unnaturally brilliant orange stripe down the middle of the back. Constant wear had removed all hair from feet, hands, and other parts frequently in contact with the ground, exposing the bright red skin.

"Maybe," said Blake, "you should leave it alone so it will recover rapidly. They really are more pleasant to look at when they are invisible."

"Could you tie that thing up somehow, Terruns, so we can experiment on it?" asked Penton wearily. "I have an idea that we'll have to hunt for our ship."

"Oh, yes. The medical staff is here, by the way. I'll tie it up, you can get out of the water, and they will strap you up more comfortably."

"You're sure that ship is gone? I don't see how a *krull* could move it."

"Not one *krull*. A troop of *krull*. We always fasten down anything movable. Even stones. They love to put them in the street, and sit on them. Very exciting crashes. A troop of *krull*, I'm afraid—but they won't carry it more than five miles or so. They lose interest quickly."

"Penton," said Blake softly, "you know, I left the liftdrive on seven-eighths, so the ship wouldn't mar the turf. I'll bet we are here three months looking for that blasted thing. Five miles and an invisible ship. More fun—"

"I'd take you up on that bet, Blake, but for one thing. I *know* we won't be here three months looking for it."

"Why?"

"Because we have emergency rations in the suits for only one week, and they use a mixture of copper selenate and potassium arsenate for fertilizer on the local crops. Laugh that off."

"You left out potassium cyanide," Blake groaned.

"I didn't leave out cyanide; that's about the only poison they don't use. All their plants want nice heavy metals like lead and copper and mercury. For non-metals they prefer the heavy ones like selenium and telurium and arsenic. This world, it would seem, is lousy with heavy metals, and so are the plants. And due to a sad neglect in my education, I never learned to digest those compounds."

IV. END OF THE KRULL

Blake looked down at himself thoughtfully. Elastic bandages wound in puttee fashion about each leg joined and wound up on his abdomen to his chest. He squeaked faintly when he moved.

"Did they give you the oil can, Ted?"

"No. But this should make a good shock-absorber. Step on it, will you? There's a chauffeur waiting to take us down to the Powers and Mechanisms Building again. Terruns said he'd meet us there."

"The bird that wrapped me ought to make a living as a mummy-maker. Did Terruns say how they go about looking for lost things?"

"Their search methods are simple and ineffective; gang of men with a long rope between them. Hurry up; I'll wait outside."

Half an hour later they joined Terruns at his office, slightly jittery, but somewhat to their own surprise, in one piece. Terruns, they had learned during this last ride, was a careful driver, indeed, for a Pornan.

"Ah. The Terrestrials," he greeted them. "Sit down." Terruns waved them to a seat with one hand. Thoughtfully, Penton noticed that Terruns' desk was of a rich, red wood finished with brightly chromium plated fixtures of quite familiar design.

"If," said Penton softly, "we don't find that ship in about three weeks we'll be gone, because we use food faster here. I've already eaten twice of those emergency rations."

"Feeding," acknowledged Blake unhappily, "but not filling. If you hear me grumble, it's my stomach, over which I'm losing all control. It is distinctly annoyed at what it righteously considers my perfidy. That one-inch lump of extinct sawdust, labeled 'one sirloin steak, 350 cal.', didn't fool it a bit. It's just as hungry as ever."

Penton nodded at a luscious-looking dark violet fruit that Terruns was toying with.

"If you ate that, Blake, your stomach would quiet down almost at once. Certainly within two hours. On Earth we mine ore that doesn't assay as high a mercury content as that thing has. Shut up and let me think."

"Why don't you rig up a radio doodle-bug?" suggested Blake. "The inductance of the ship should be darned easy to spot, and working the way they do with those—"

"Doodle-bugs are out," sighed Penton, "I thought of that. They're fine for finding buried metal, but they have two troubles here. Pornans broadcast power, which I have studied carefully while you were studying their ore-handling machinery. But they do not use radio methods. I gave Terruns complete data on radio. In six months or a year he'll make an effective radio tube, I'll bet.

"If you want to wait for that—in the meantime all our tools are in the ship. The electrical field method doesn't work because that requires an amplifier. The magnetic induction won't work till we are already so near you'd find it quicker with the rope method they use."

"Yes," sighed Penton, "but no ship." Blake turned to Terruns.

"How long will it take them to run that search out to that five mile circle?" he asked.

"Ah," said Terruns hesitantly, glancing at some sheets in front of him, "two months and three days, the last time. But more men this time. A month, perhaps? Not quick enough—I'm truly sorry, but you have no idea how annoying these creatures are to a decent, civilized—"

"Stomach," suggested Blake unhappily. "We're rapidly finding out. You've no idea how annoyed we'll be as we slowly starve to death. Oh, no idea."

Penton interrupted.

"Listen," he begged Blake, "will you eat that fruit over there and shut up one way or another? I'm trying to think. There must be some way—this thing's gone on too damned long now."

"Oh, yes, much," agreed Terruns. "Were doing all we can—"

"I know. We're not blaming you or your people." Penton grinned. "You are doing your damnedest, I realize, but the thing's senseless. There must be some way to stop them. This world of yours is too monotonous for your own good. Always warm, everywhere. Always light, every—yeah. So it is. Sweet—Terruns!"

Suddenly Penton jumped out of his seat with all the speed of a Pornan, his hand flashing back to his pack. Abruptly his hand was leveling a short, lensed tube at Terruns' startled face. The Pornan first bent back in his chair hastily in startled amazement, then, thinking the tube a weapon, his hand darted out like a striking snake to twist the cold, crystalline eye of the tube away from him.

Penton dropped his tube with a howl of pain and leaped back, shaking his hand, but grinning sheepishly.

"Sorry, Terruns, must have startled you," he apologized. "Look—it's harmless—just a light." Again he picked up the tube, in his left hand this time, and turned it on Blake. The brilliant light beam of his atomic flashlight stabbed sharply into Blake's face forcing him to blink, squinting until his eyes became adjusted.

"Yes," said Terruns, uncertainly. "Most—er—confusing. Your thoughts are not at all clear."

Penton turned the beam of light into Terruns' face. The Pornan shut his eyes at once, throwing a hand up to his face.

"It's very brilliant, uncomfortably so. Could you turn—turn it somewhere else—oh. Yes, turn it away."

Penton turned away the light with a sigh of relief.

"That, Terruns, is all I want to know. Look, take these, and make 'em fit somehow. And come on, we're due for some good hunting." Penton passed over a pair of space goggles, and reluctantly Terruns adjusted them to his face.

"It's an unpleasant sensation," he told the explorers. "But, yes, I think, my friend, that you have solved, with your other-world mind a long outstanding problem. Just one moment and we will be on our way. Oh, do you have another pair for my friend, Drunath, a very excellent gentleman? Spent his life finding quicker ways to kill *krull*. Just down the hall—"

Blake passed over his set of space goggles in blank wonderment. Presently the four started down, and out of the building, into a side street that Terruns recommended for a test. The test was wholly inconclusive.

"The park," said Drunath slowly, "is always infested with *krull*. There is a wood, a group of trees, that has not been properly searched in fifty years. Ropes cannot be used. Shall we go there?"

Half an hour later, cars had deposited them, together with a troop of Drunath's extermination squad. Penton and Blake, for the first time, had an opportunity to walk through the spot where the ship should have been, a remembered swale between a little hillock of pink turf and a vine-covered outthrust of black, glistening rock. It rose some hundred feet to a huge, rugged boulder that looked strangely like a lopeared *krull* with an ugly, grinning face.

"*Krull* Rock," explained Drunath. "Always search it first for anything smaller than an automobile. If there aren't any *krull* there, there aren't any in town."

Blake looked up. Black rock, jumbled boulders, and creeping vines. Bright metal testified to a complete ring of steel traps, all unoccupied. Penton was working with his flash, adjusting the tiny atomic generator it contained to maximum power. Then he pressed the little button.

A low hum came from the instrument, then a shaft of light unbearable, corruscating brilliance. It shimmered from the black rocks in a scintillating, twinkling rain—and vanished as Penton released the flash. Slowly, Blake's eyes adjusted themselves. Then again the flash, and again, till it was on full, and Blake's eyes had readjusted to its light.

Penton was chuckling softly. The air was full of soft whimpers, and little screeches. They turned to howls of dismay as Penton and Blake, unsteady for laughter, picked off dozens of the crazy-quilt *krull*. Their UV pistols working methodically, they cleaned out the entire colony of the beasts perched on the rock.

Slowly, unsteadily, Terruns and Drunath were firing.

"Curse all Gods, destroy all devils, and particular maledictions of *krull*," Drunath exclaimed. "Your goggles are inadequate. I can hardly see through them. For the first time in my life I can dimly see a colony, a whole troop of *krull*, and I cannot shoot straight!" Drunath threw down his weapon in disgust. "Can you," asked Blake, "see what is on top of that blasted rock?"

"Fire. It looks like fire to us."

"Not fire. Metal. A whole metal ship. Your idiotic krull didn't carry it two hundred yards, but just up above where your search methods weren't worth a damn. We will move it."

"You are leaving?" asked Terruns sadly.

"Not," Penton assured him, "by six planets and a dozen moons. We're staying for the shooting. And, oh, my friends, what royal and unadulterated joy I'll take in running the last of those *krull* out of this town." Penton and Blake lifted simultaneously into the air, and within a few seconds into the ship.

Alone in their spaceship a day later, Blake puffed complacently at a cigarette.

"I would still like to know just how you thought of it. It's an excellent way, I don't dispute, but how did you figure it out, Ted?"

Penton smiled affably.

"What big eyes you have, Terruns. The better to see with five billion miles from the sun. Look, Rod, though their eyes are extremely sensitive, they are powerfully weak in accommodation. The inhabitants on this satellite never have any real light out here. I was using a light so powerful that these unadapted fellows just couldn't see in it at all; we could, after a moment. But the *krull* were totally blinded by it, and suffered acute pain in the bargain. It's not surprising that an animal that depends so on its eyes should be paralyzed when its eyes won't work. When I flashed the light they could not wiggle a muscle, they were so scared. And they couldn't keep the ship invisible, either!"

"Nor," said Blake comfortably, "our food supply."

www.ingramcontent.com/pod-product-compliance
Lightning Source LLC
Chambersburg PA
CBHW011448170626
46816CB00008B/2580